PEARLCASTING

A love story

Lynn Matheson

Copyright © 2016 Lynn Matheson
All rights reserved.

ISBN: 1496099834
ISBN 13: 9781496099839

CHAPTER ONE

He came with the snow.
It was the first day of the spring term with no sign of spring. The snow had arrived unexpectedly and banked itself in pillows all over the grounds. It had lain down on the rooftops and blocked up the gutterings. It had crept silently along the footpaths and invited itself onto the window ledges, blanketing the rugby pitches two feet thick. It had silenced even the constant *ack, ack* of the resident crows. The fir trees lining the drive were drooping with its weight, tired and old. Orla knew how they felt. She guided the little red Mini forward gingerly. What was it for snow? Low or high gear? She could not remember. She tried low gear, inching forward, hardly moving.

"Don't slide," she told herself sternly.

Just before the main building, there was a line of cars: four-by-fours ground to a halt on the ice. They were blocking Orla's path, as impregnable as a wall, preventing any further movement forward. The cars reminded Orla of military vehicles: ugly, brutal things you would use in a war rather than to bring children to school.

She regarded cars as a necessary evil. An impossibly thin woman with blond hair had alighted from one of them and was having an animated discussion with a stout, bald man in front. They were dressed in that country set style so beloved by most of the parents: all shiny new Barbours and Hunter Wellingtons without a hint of mud. Orla recognised them both vaguely. They were businesspeople, originally from London, now playing at Suffolk rural life. She had noticed that in the main the mothers were always thin to the point of being skeletal while the men just let themselves go to seed, enjoying their good fortune by eating and drinking or perhaps comforting themselves, hiding from their unhappiness. Orla herself fell between these two extremes. She imagined it must be quite miserable to keep yourself that thin, though she did admire the result and wished she had the willpower to lose a few pounds. The woman was perfectly coiffed, even at this hour of the morning, with full makeup and hair tied up in a perfect chignon. This level of grooming was another thing Orla had never been able to manage. The man, typical of his type, held no interest for her. She didn't find seriously overweight people at all attractive, though she felt guilty for this. She was sure they had their reasons. Usually, the men were pretty boring to talk to—self-satisfied and arrogant.

Don't mind me, I only work here, thought Orla.

She felt a flash of anger at them for stopping her progress, and a familiar resentment and distaste for the parents rose within her. Why did they have to drive the biggest, most gas-guzzling cars available? Hadn't they heard of global warming? The parents appeared to be in constant competition with each other for status in material things. Cars were one of the ways they could show off their wealth. Orla had never sought riches. She had chosen teaching, as she thought it would give her meaning. She had wanted at some distant point in the past to be a good person, to do worthy deeds in the world, to make a difference. She had hoped to find fulfilment in her career. She had not achieved this. Part of her had a suspicion that perhaps the acquisitive parents were right all along. Perhaps she should have sought wealth rather than more lofty ideals. Orla knew though that many of the school's clients were far from happy. Divorce was common. Money had not given them contentment. Many of them seemed to be in a permanent state of unease, desperate for their rather ordinary children to shine at something. Being ordinary was no longer good enough. She felt guilty for her grouchy thoughts. Mornings made her feel like that these days. Some of the parents were actually very pleasant to her, even calling her inspirational. And so she was, in spite of herself. Orla had a gift for interesting children in writing and appreciating poetry. She was hard on herself though and never felt she achieved enough. She was not really aware of the effect she had on the boys she taught and how they remembered her lessons with fondness for years afterwards. She abandoned the car at the side of the drive and tramped determinedly towards the school in her new leather boots, which crunched pleasantly on the snow. She looked down at her boots admiringly and felt her spirits lift a little. The air was biting with the cold, but there was little wind. The winter day was perfect in its muffled beauty, but she was oblivious to it, wrapped in her own thoughts.

Orla rounded the bend and there it was: Northwold. It was, like many others, a grand eighteenth-century country house that had been converted into a second-rank boarding school for children of the military and the aspiring newly wealthy in 1935. The house had been remodelled in 1900 in a baroque, showy Italian style by the last aristocrat who had bought it: the Earl of Cardean. A stone balustrade with urns above topped the main doorway. Above those was an asymmetrical tower with a square, copper-roofed cupola. On the death of the earl, it had been sold to pay death duties. Northwold had no reputation, no entry requirements, and little to recommend it other than the knowledge that one's children did not have to mix with the hoi polloi of East Anglia. The local state schools outperformed it in examination results every year. Northwold had ideas above its station, just like most of the nouveau riche who sent their children to it. Apart from RAF and army families, most of the school's clientele were local businesspeople: self-made millionaires from gravel, climbing frames, property development, leather goods, scrap metal, hucksterism, security—the strangest things made money. There were also some Ukrainians whose fathers paid their school fees with suitcases of money, and some dark-eyed Spanish boys with better manners than the homegrown youth. In spite of the school advertising itself as boarding, the actual boarders were few in number. Most of the boys went home at weekends, and some were day pupils only. Most people now seemed to regard the practice of boarding out your children from the age of seven as barbaric. Orla would tend to agree with them. Northwold was unusual in that it had resisted the conversion to coed: it catered only to the male of the species. The house was fine enough, but Orla missed the baronial architecture of her native Scotland. What was a grand house without a turret, faux battlements, and impossible towered rooms? It was no Glamis Castle. She missed the Disneyscape of Edinburgh where she had been educated, or half educated, to be more accurate. Orla's grandmother had been in service at Glamis at one time, and Orla reflected that nothing much had changed. In spite of her university education, Orla was still just a servant to rich people.

Orla bypassed the main gate and headed for the side entrance. The English Department was hidden away in the old stable block at the back, as dusty and neglected as the ragged books the children were issued. She ascended the stairs as if to a gallows, barely noticing the peeling woodwork and the dirty, threadbare carpets. Orla had grown used to the shabbiness of her surroundings. She caught sight of herself reflected in the window. She was small—tiny, in fact, not quite scraping five feet. Her hair was long and dark blond. She wore it for school in a rather staid plait, which fell down her shoulder almost to her waist. Her hair would never quite stay in place, and tendrils escaped from their prison throughout the day. If she ever wore it loose, there were comments from the older members of staff and the old at heart. So she toed the line…a little. She wore very little makeup: mascara, a little lipstick. Orla tried to act the schoolmistress, though inside it was not who she was. She had never been…not inside. She was thirty-five but looked much younger. Orla felt worn from her work, but as yet this did not show in her face, which was still free from lines. Her features were small, her cheekbones high, and her eyes large and green with long, childlike lashes. Orla was striking, beautiful even, though she was unaware of this fact and had always been. She had been brought up by old-fashioned Scots with a certain dourness about them. Orla had never been complimented on her looks by her parents. They would regard such a thing as vanity, frivolity. She had an out-of-fashion figure: full and feminine, not skinny. She had been pitifully thin as a child, but in adulthood she had blossomed with a womanly shape: curvaceous. She was like a 1950s pinup girl with an hourglass figure. She did not act her age. She still liked to giggle and do silly things on occasion. These qualities, of course, endeared her to the boys, who treated her almost as one of them. They entrusted her with their secrets: girlfriends, biological worries, difficult parental relationships. Orla was the recipient of a thousand confidences.

Usually, she could not help them.

She entered her classroom, heaving the door open with her shoulder because the handle did not work properly. The room was cold, as cold as outside. She flipped on the heater switch, but it would take hours to warm the high-ceilinged room. She had brought the heater herself from home. The ancient oil-fired radiators were not up to the task. They were turned on late and switched off early.

Orla could see her breath in front of her as she sighed heavily. She arranged a few things listlessly on her desk. Orla had tried hard to brighten the room. She had displays of work in primary colours and inspirational posters to cover up the dirty magnolia paint. The wooden desks were arranged in rows, but the classes were now so large they were squashed together with no room to walk easily between them. The computer on her desk was dated. She paused for a small prayer of desperation: *Please make this term better than the last one. Make things go right. Just this once.*

Orla decided on coffee. This meant braving the common room, but her need for caffeine was greater than her dread of social interaction with the staff. She was scarred with the little jibes against her: she was too loud, too happy, too sad, too Scottish, too intellectual, too popular with the children, too Roman Catholic…just *too*. She was real, not a shell, not a ghost. That was what they really didn't like. Brooding on these thoughts, she headed back outside to the main building.

Outside the office was when she saw him.

He was standing outside the headmaster's study, looking slightly awkward and out of place, adjusting to the new uniform, fingering the stiff collar repeatedly. He smiled at Orla broadly—too confidently, she thought—but it was possibly bravado to mask the nerves of the new boy. He was about fifteen and as promising a specimen of humanity as any. He had white-blond hair, unusually very closely cropped, as this was not the fashion of the school. The usual game was to grow it out as long as possible without being marched forcibly into town to the barber. His tanned skin was a warm brown, and his turquoise eyes were wide and clear. They seemed like the eyes of a much younger child, giving a boyish quality to the face, which was at odds with his six-foot-tall frame and already expanding chest. He was halfway between boy and man. Orla guessed he was from German or Nordic ancestry. She recognised the features, as her own mother was Norwegian originally. She felt a contraction deep in her abdomen as she looked at him. She was surprised. This usually happened when she looked at stunningly attractive adult men. It had not, in fact, happened to her for a very long time—certainly not since she had moved to rural Suffolk. It was like a visceral animal reaction to a thing of beauty. He reminded her of someone else. Someone she had known long ago. He was perfectly beautiful. He made her think of the marble statue of Eros she had seen in the museum in Naples. She had looked at it for a long time. The Romans had not been afraid of the body, afraid of beauty. Orla dismissed the strange feeling with a slight sense of unease. She had trained herself to be almost professional at school…to act a part, not really to allow herself to be. Her mind registered him as a pupil, but an older, more primal part of herself had told her something else. Strange. After all, the school almost specialised in good-looking, Aryan sporty boys. They didn't usually have any effect on her.

She managed a brisk, "Good morning."

His reply explained the haircut and the unease with the uniform. He had a slight American twang.

"Morning, ma'am." He greeted her with a wide smile.

Orla's eyes shone with amusement at the unfamiliar word. She tilted her head back and laughed.

"There's no need to call me that. I am not one hundred and five!" she replied in mock severity.

He would no doubt find the transition to English public school life difficult. Orla resolved to help him in her "I am everybody's maidservant" kind of way. She breezed past him and was surprised as she turned to enter the common room to see his eyes still intently looking after her, looking right into her, as if he could see all of her secrets. The eyes seemed to be almost laughing at her, not unkindly but with affectionate amusement. Slightly rattled, she pushed her way into the staff cocoon and waited in the interminable coffee queue.

Yes, he came, unexpectedly, with the snow.

CHAPTER TWO

The day began with morning service in the Hall. It was a nondescript room lined with dark wood that formed part of the 1930s boarding house, with long windows, which wouldn't open, leading to a stuffy, overheated atmosphere. Occasionally, one of the boys would faint from a combination of high temperature and boredom. At one end of the room there was a badly painted portrait of the old headmaster, and at the other endless photographs of boarders from years gone by. As the photographs became more modern, the numbers of pupils dwindled; boarding had begun to be seen as old-fashioned, even cruel by many, modern people. The school did possess a lovely little ornate chapel on the grounds, which had been built at the same time as the main house, but it was not big enough to take all of the boys, so they squashed in to the Hall, where a table with a cross placed on it pretended to be the altar. The heavy brass cross had mysteriously gone missing last term and then just as mysteriously reappeared on the last day. The reverend Bunting had been furious. He looked at Orla with the sort of look that suggested she was a suspect: somewhere between hatred and contempt. Orla looked back fearlessly with what she hoped was the same sentiment. She disliked him intensely, as did nearly everybody else. He was an Anglican, a sect of Christianity that Orla could not fathom. She had asked everyone what Anglicans actually believed in and had received no satisfactory answer. She suspected he was an atheist. His sermons had no religious content. Often they concerned a dog with a stammer and an eagle that did its business on people's unsuspecting heads at moments throughout the story. Orla wondered what a child with a stammer would make of the characterisation. Fortunately, there were no boys with stammers at Northwold to be offended by the vicar. The boys laughed in all the right places, but Orla could never work out what these stories were supposed to be about, and she did not enjoy the crude humour. It was Christianity that was very careful never to mention God. Reverend Bunting was tall with an enormous gut caused by the sin of gluttony, and he constantly mentioned that he used to work in a bank, as if he was somehow ashamed of being a priest. He was divorced and remarried to a large, blond woman, which apparently meant he was not allowed to have a parish, so he had to make do with a school. He didn't look happy about it.

Finally, the reverend stopped talking, and then came the hymns. To Orla, this was the best part of the day. She loved to sing and tried to stand next to the head of maths, David Pinfold, so she could enjoy his fine tenor. He was pompous, snobbish, and unworldly, but Orla still managed to quite like him, if only because he was the least of all evils. He had been something in the RAF and had a fixed, out-of-date view of the world, where everyone knew their place. He was sniffy about the newly acquired wealth of many of the families and referred to the farming dynasties as the "real thing." Orla could not see how they were any more real than anyone else. Their children tended not to be very bright and to have a very high opinion of themselves. The endless layers of English society irritated Orla. She regarded them as ridiculous and dated. Northwold was the right place for archaic views. David tried to patronise Orla, whom he definitely regarded as *not* the real thing; he was miffed to discover that she had an MA from Edinburgh, which in his world rather trumped his being from Salford. One day standing next to him, Orla had noticed that he appeared to have completely hairless arms. She wondered if he was hairless all over his body. Today she was jammed in between Jack Debden, who could not hold a note, and Harriet Farringdon, who could not sing either but thought she could. Still, Orla felt her spirits lift as they ambled through "A Knight Won His Spurs." Most of the boys detested singing and were largely inaudible, in contrast to the staff, whose voices boomed out across the gap between them and the pupils. Orla allowed herself to think about Jack for a while. He was very young, just out of university and incredibly good humoured and pleasant. Orla liked him very much but didn't think he would stick it out long. He was already showing signs of disaffection. Though she liked him, she couldn't exactly say she was attracted to him. She wasn't. He had that kind of asexuality that lots of sweet men had. He just didn't do anything to her inside. In spite of this, she sometimes fantasised about having a relationship with him, getting married, running a little school in sleepy, affectionate, easygoing bliss. She knew this was not going to happen. He was far too young for her, and in fact he had a pretty Spanish girlfriend who appeared to boss him around a fair bit and had plans for matrimony. Orla stopped dreaming and brought her attention back to her prosaic surroundings. She spent a few moments idly watching the dust motes as they danced in the air. She noted the freshness of the boys as opposed to the worn faces of the staff. How sad it was that one day the boys would turn into such people themselves: they would lose their sense of fun and their joy and become cruel, cold, hard, ugly.

Then an awkward thing happened.

The music master, Heathcote-Jones, abruptly stopped playing the piano and bellowed out at one of the upper thirds: Fraser. Apparently, his sin had been that he was not singing. In fact, a good 80 percent of the upper third had not been singing, as well as 90 percent of the lower third. Fraser had been singled out for no obvious reason. Fraser was always in trouble and had achieved the feat of being in detention ten times last term, which was impressive as there were only ten weeks in the term. Orla had tried hard to understand his behaviour, but she couldn't quite work him out. She supposed that if the school had not been so desperate for money, he would have been sent away long ago. He could be a bully but was incredibly funny and very adept at cheering Orla up. As with all bullies, there was something wrong at the root—but what was it? Fraser was blond and slightly tubby, with pudgy cheeks and slightly hooded eyes, which seemed to suggest he had already grown wary and weary of the world. As Orla watched him, she was reminded of his disgrace last term. He had teased a handicapped boy from another school during a sports fixture, scribbling on his journal and calling him names during the match. The headmaster of the other school had been furious and refused to play against Northwold again. The school's name was now mud to him, not for the first time. Orla could not understand such unkindness from Fraser. Neither could anyone else. Nobody knew what to do about it. Fraser continued as usual. A detention had not made any difference. It never would. Nothing ever made any difference.

Heathcote-Jones bellowed for a good three minutes and then made Fraser sing the next verse on his own. The child went pink, opened his mouth, shut it again, exhaled, and then reedily managed to do as he was asked. The embarrassment in the Hall was palpable among both pupils and staff. Orla was aware of several of the boys looking sideways at her to gauge her reaction. She tried and failed to effect an impassable expression.

Orla was internally furious. She felt the anger rising in her like a tsunami: vast and unstoppable, but, unlike the tsunami, there was no outlet for Orla's rage, nowhere for it to flow to. This kind of event was the cause of Orla's stress. She had used to be a happy, easygoing person, but the injustices of the school had worn her down. These days, fury came quickly to her. The head of the Prep Department had distinctly told everyone last term that shouting at the children was not allowed, as it lowered their self-esteem, according to him. Orla was of the view that most of them had too much self-esteem, but that was by the by. One of her few almost friends on the staff had been unceremoniously sacked last year for using the word *pathetic* to a child. She had actually said, "Stop being so pathetic and get into groups." A parent had complained. This was used as an excuse to get rid of her. The real reason was that she was a woman of strong opinions, and the headmaster had some strange fear of such women that resulted in misogyny. It was true that Rita Henderson, the sacked teacher, could be harsh, but she got good results—and ultimately she did care about the children and their progress. Most schools would have been glad to have her. Orla felt she herself was too soft. She didn't have it in her to go for the jugular, and the boys knew it. She tried for the praise and encouragement tack, but it didn't always work. Orla was next on the list of people to intimidate until they threw in the towel. Orla had no idea why the new head of prep, Neil Blenkinsopp, seemed to hate her so much. He was making a habit of belittling her. Blenkinsopp was originally from Yorkshire, apparently originally a miner's son who was now puffed up with his own importance and largely devoid of humour. As Orla listened to Heathcote-Jones shouting, the slights committed against her came into her mind. On one particular occasion, she had been sitting in the common room telling a mildly funny story about not being able to find some sports equipment for a club she had been asked to stand in for at the last minute. His response was to ask her how she had ever got through teaching practice in front of a room full of staff. Orla had been furious and fired off an ill-considered email to him on return to her room. Though he had apologised, she sensed it was not sincere and the first sign of the start of his bullying regime.

As usual, it was one rule for the men and one for the women. Here was Heathcote-Jones getting away with murder as he always did. Rules were bent for him. Orla herself had been keelhauled for raising her voice last term, upsetting a particularly delicate flower of East Anglian youth. What he had done to cause her to do this was of course not mentioned. The parents of the day pupils were constant complainers, getting their money's worth.

Staff came and went. Orla remained.

It was no secret there was no love lost between her and Heathcote-Jones. He was supposedly named Humphrey Heathcote-Jones, but Orla had a suspicion it was an assumed name. The pretension went with everything else about him. Today he was sporting a full tweed suit, which he'd had to get specially made on account of his enormous girth. He was short and balding and wore tiny brown-rimmed glasses. He was often found wandering around the grounds blowing a hunting horn or mowing down children in his ancient Jaguar. Heathcote-Jones referred to his car as his fanny-magnet. What kind of fanny would be attracted to him and the decrepit lump of metal Orla could not imagine. He seemed to wish to give the impression of an English aristocrat, but the effect was more Mr Toad of Toad Hall. Orla found him odious. He had made several failed passes at her, so these days his conversation alternated between crude flirtation and insults. Last term alone, Orla had had to endure him asking her to go into a dark room with him to "discuss" some planning, calling her a dragon, comparing her to a particularly unattractive woman in a children's film, and sitting too close to her on the boarding house sofa and then leaping away when someone came by. Orla was so tired of it. In other modern workplaces, he would have been at least disciplined for sexual harassment, but at Northwold such things were never mentioned. The school values in this area had not advanced beyond the Edwardian era. He did as he pleased. Rumour had it he had deflowered the French assistant, a lonely eighteen-year-old, in the boarding house office. Bizarrely, he was quite popular with a section of the younger children and some of the more gullible parents. Orla found him to be completely fake. Over the years, she had discovered that his father had been a tabloid journalist and he had been born in Harlow, gone to comprehensive school, and left with no qualifications, but the country squire act seemed to be important to him. She found him petty, vindictive, gossipy, and sexually suspect. No doubt he was taking revenge on Fraser for some minor infraction. Finally, the ordeal was over.

Orla bluffed her way through the first two lessons somehow or other—the practically unteachable lower third. She had been given all of the bottom set English classes this year. It was part of the edging-her-out strategy. The idea was to make her so unhappy that she left of her own volition. Some of the boys could barely read. It was her job to get them through the Common Entrance exam into the more ethereal surroundings of Westminster, St Paul's, or Eton. It wasn't going to happen. It was a task nobody would have been able to manage. A few academically gifted students achieved this rare feat each year, but most had to content themselves with staying at Northwold, much to the disappointment of their parents. Orla would get the blame. She rarely did any lesson planning these days. She had realised that nobody cared if you did any or not, so she had long since stopped bothering. There had been a time when she had been conscientious. She had been a believer. Orla had overhauled the English Department single-handedly. She had devised new schemes of work for every year group, organised the readers and bought more with her own money, and modelled modern techniques using ICT, images, film, drama, and oral work to drag the curriculum into the current world, not the world of Tom Brown's school days. All of this had been unappreciated by the management, and when the idle South African head of English had left for greener pastures, the promotion was given to Anthony De Bois, an ex-solicitor with two years of experience of teaching the upper first only. Orla realised she had wasted her time playing the game. She knew she was supposed to find enough fulfilment from helping the children succeed, but she had always been ambitious. She had wanted to become management so she could make a bigger difference, have influence on policy, bring her own ideas forward rather than just following someone else's.

But it wasn't to be. She was devastated.

She was now becoming disillusioned with the process of teaching itself. The intelligent children did well whether they were taught with skill or taught badly. The teaching made little difference. The less well-endowed with brains did badly however hard she tried to get them to understand. They exhausted her. She came to believe her role was pointless. This was not really the case, but Orla, in her misery and despair, could not see the effects she had, effects that were not measurable by examinations or noticed by narrow-minded headmasters.

Not much work had taken place in Orla's first lesson. The boys were full of their Christmas holidays, bursting to tell her their winter sun adventures. Most had been skiing and had sundry broken limbs as evidence. Some had lounged on Egyptian or Indian beaches. They bragged and point-scored off each other, ribbing each other mercilessly. To most of them, English was just a boring interlude between rugby matches, something to be endured. Some of the more precious parents complained about the more raucous members of the class as bullies. To Orla, it was just the way things were. Boys had always done this. Times had changed though, and she was supposed to write down each incident in triplicate and report it to the deputy head. She didn't. Orla was always in trouble for not following policies. She didn't believe in them and preferred to use her own intuition as to how to react to situations. Blenkinsopp told her she was a maverick and that he too had once been a maverick. Orla did not believe him on both counts.

Halfway through the double period, Orla found her eyes resting on little Rupert. Oblivious to the din all around him, he was diligently working on the snow description work she had set, carefully checking his spellings in the dictionary and using the thesaurus correctly as she had demonstrated at the beginning of the lesson. He was the only one doing so. It would be safe to say Rupert did not fit in. He was old money—inherited wealth. He had a myriad of undiagnosed learning difficulties, and he rarely spoke. Orla felt a chink of sunshine enter the blind of her mind for the first time that morning. She felt a surge of maternal love for him: her little lost soul. Orla approached his desk and gave him her most encouraging smile.

"What did you do over Christmas, Rupert?" she asked gently.

He raised his head slowly. He was tiny, thin, and pale, like the runt of a litter of pups. He had coal-black hair, poker straight. Rupert smiled nervously at her.

"We didn't do much. My mum's got depression," he managed.

There was a hiatus of silence in the room as the other boys took in the information that Rupert had actually said something and then the bizarre nature of what he had vouchsafed. The calm was shattered by James, rugby scholar and general boor, who guffawed loudly. This set them all off, giggling helplessly, clapping their hands and whooping.

Orla flared at the unkindness. She backed to the front of the room and proceeded to rant at their manners for five minutes. She didn't know what she was saying. She opened her mouth and words came out. They all looked suitably sheepish. They didn't like to upset her, not really. Orla pulled herself together for the last few minutes. She showed them a DVD clip of Narnia and then wrote a quick description of it on the smartboard. The smartboard was the one piece of modern equipment in Orla's room, and she made good use of it. Some of the more elderly members of staff professed that they did not know how to use theirs, so the money they had cost was wasted. It was typical that training had not been provided. Orla had just taught herself. She could see James, out of the corner of her eye, who had not done a tap of work for the whole lesson, copying her words down verbatim—which she had expressly said not to do—and then finishing off by sketching an elaborate love heart underneath with the legend "I love you" scrawled across it. Orla knew that he hoped this would melt her enough not to give him an E grade again this term.

It would not melt her.

Break was a welcome respite of hot coffee, biscuits, and the warmth of the common room radiator. Lemon-faced Mrs Roebuck had already irritated her.

"I was just passing your room, Miss McKenzie," she announced shrilly. "What a noise. Was it a drama lesson?"

Orla, for once, could not be bothered to enter the duel. She had crossed swords with the woman many times before. Thelma Roebuck represented the type of schoolteacher that she loathed. She was a derelict, decayed, dried-up stick who had nothing good to say about anyone. She looked the epitome of the sensible, dull schoolteacher with black trousers, clumpy flat shoes, and a faded brown cardigan. Orla imagined she had bought the entire ensemble from the dowdy town department store ten years ago. Her hair was short—of course—for practicality, and her lined face was crowned with a worn-looking pair of steel-rimmed spectacles. James shared Orla's opinion. One morning, he had announced, "Mrs Roebuck, there's a face you want to punch!" Orla smiled at the recollection of the unkind but accurate remark. How had Orla ended up with such a group of grotesques as the staff? She didn't know. She had a horror of turning into one of them. She imagined other schools full of fresh-faced, earnest young women diligently planning outstanding lessons while wearing prim cardigans. If such places existed, they probably wouldn't employ Orla. Discipline, or the lack of it, was a running sore in the school. Since Blenkinsopp's arrival and his weak, insecure fear of parental complaint, the staff had been deterred from telling anybody off. The result was bedlam. Orla actually had better behaviour in her lessons than most of the staff due to her popularity and reputation for being entertaining. It was Blenkinsopp's first headship, and he was making a pig's ear of it. He was being bullied by the high master above him to improve results, so he in turn bullied those below him. And then most of the staff in their turn bullied the boys. The boys bullied each other. So it went in such badly run organisations.

Orla gave the Roebuck a hard look, turned away, and listened to the conversations around her.

"I see David Elliott's mother has run off with a toy boy." This was from Dana Peck, the French teacher. She was similar in many ways to the Roebuck: elderly, divorced, ugly, old, bitter. Orla could not stand her habit of picking on some of the more sensitive children and belittling them. At the moment, it was a delicate Jewish boy called Daniel. She wondered if Dana was really anti-Semitic. It seemed difficult to believe, but it was hard to find another explanation for her dislike of such a lovely child.

"Really?" The Roebuck leaned in to hear more.

Gossip, endless gossip, doing people down.

"Well, she said to me, their eyes met across a crowded room and they just knew. He's fifteen years her junior. I mean really. What about David? What about the children?"

Orla bristled at the faux concern for the children's welfare. This was the reason women were not supposed to get divorced, were not supposed to be happy. Think of the children! As if they could be happy with two parents who obviously weren't. Orla felt a gush of admiration for Mrs Elliott, taking the bit between her teeth, striding out into a new life with her toy boy. How absolutely wonderful! Orla's overactive imagination pictured Mrs Elliott with some muscled male model, laughing and splashing each other with water on a white sand beach, having left the straitjacket of East Anglian upper-middle-class society far behind.

The earnest art teacher, Charlotte Winter, tried to see both sides. She was in a state of permanent misery, and Orla had noticed antidepressants poking out of her voluminous handbag.

"But surely if she has been in a loveless marriage all those years..." She trailed off after a withering look from the Roebuck.

"Good on her, I say," Orla said. "Take your chances where you can find them."

The female staff regarded her in silence. Orla had the feeling she had broken some kind of woman taboo. She was not thinking of the children, of duty, of worthiness. The male staff were up at the other end discussing their latest golf match. They used sport as a way of bonding and ostracising the women. Orla had at one time in a fit of enthusiasm joined the local club with the school corporate membership, but nobody had ever asked her to play. She had given up on it as a bad idea. She was not the golfing type. In her daydreams she was more the "go-go dancing on a tabletop in Soho" type.

She got up and returned to her corridor. As she arrived at her door, the upper third were lining up shabbily along the wall: her next class. Orla saw *the* new boy at the front of the line. She felt a slight queasy panic rising from the pit of her stomach. His face visibly lightened when he saw who the teacher was.

"Morning, Miss McKenzie," he drawled and gave her his best smile.

Orla realised he had managed to learn her name since their first encounter. What was he doing here? Surely he was too old for this class. The unsettled feeling he had created in her earlier returned.

"I thought you were in the upper fourth," snapped Orla at him. "You must be in the wrong place."

Orla didn't know what form he was actually in, and she realised she had spoken to him far too sharply. She felt herself going slightly pink. His face darkened almost comically.

"Er...well, yes, I am Ma—I mean Miss—but Miss Snowdon said she thought I was better here because I don't know the curriculum and...I'm not very good at English," he tailed off lamely.

Orla could see tears starting to prick at the back of his eyes. She felt guilty and recovered herself enough to make soothing noises about how everything was fine and that she would find out what the case was later. Orla herded the class inside and waited for them to stand at their desks. He didn't realise this was the custom and sat down straight away. Then he noticed what the others were doing and stood up again. Orla settled them; gave out books on autopilot; ignored numerous requests to watch DVDs, do drama, or go outside for a walk; and chose someone to start the text. As the voice rumbled restfully on, Orla perched on the edge of her desk, as was her custom, half sitting and half standing. She allowed herself to think about this new dilemma. She had not imagined she would actually have to teach him. She realised she did not even know his name. The class turned the pages as noisily as they could manage, and Orla spoke.

"Perhaps the new boy could have a turn?" she questioned and looked at him with a confidence she did not feel. "What is your name?"

"Elijah Haynes," he stated and began reading. He read the page fluently, with a clear, expressive voice and intonation. Orla could not understand why he was in this class, two years down. It was a cruel thing to do. She closed her eyes momentarily and felt the frustration she often felt at Northwold building up inside her again. She breathed in deeply and exhaled, trying to calm her thoughts as the soothing, unfamiliar southern-states accent lulled her spirit. The voice was warm and rich, like black coffee, making her thoughts flit to long summer days, cotton fields, big skies, pickup trucks, and cattle drives. These things she had never seen.

Elijah Haynes.
Elijah.
Bringer of fire.

CHAPTER THREE

Orla was sitting that evening in her armchair in her kitchen, reflecting on the events of the day. The kitchen was the warmest room in her tiny cottage due to the gargantuan old Aga. Orla huddled next to it, wrapped in a plaid blanket, her hands wrapped around a mug of green tea. The room was perfectly silent. After a day of children's noise, she couldn't stand the radio nor music, which would only jangle her shredded nerves.

The cottage was semidetached, stone, with odd little arched windows and a heavy wooden door, also arched. It had only one storey, with red roof tiles. It had been built in the 1700s for farm labourers on the country estate. The door opened directly into the kitchen, which doubled as the sitting room. There was one bedroom, which had been made even smaller by being sliced in half to provide the convenience of a bathroom sometime in the 1920s. Orla had chosen the whole cottage for the sake of the bath, which was a huge monstrosity set on little feet. It was so deep it took an hour to fill from the sputtering taps. Orla loved to luxuriate in it. She liked her cottage. It was too hot in summer and too cold in winter. The windows rattled and let the wind in, and birds made nests in the holes in the roof. In the mornings, the windowsills were always soaking wet from condensation. It was like a hobbit house, a thing from a fairy tale. It suited Orla very well. Frank lived in the adjoining house. He worked as a groundskeeper at Northwold. He was big, brawny, slow, and gentle, and he had no wife. Frank left Orla gifts of skinned poached rabbits and pheasants on the stone front step, and he did little repairs to her fence and weeded her garden without being asked. In the snobbish world of the school, Frank barely registered with most of the staff. Orla loved him—not in a romantic way, but more in the real sense of the word *love* talked about in the Bible. He was like a rock under the earth: not showy, but there, necessary. Somehow, though he rarely spoke to her directly, he anchored Orla, kept her in the earth, comforted her by just existing, reminding her that not everyone was like her teaching colleagues. Some followed ancient ways. It seemed as if Frank had grown out of the ground itself, had always been part of the landscape, would always be.

She was exhausted as usual. Orla had taught a full day and then supervised the Badminton Club, though she knew nothing about badminton. Then boarders' supper and boarders' prep duty until seven. She had had no breaks today, supervising break time in the morning and then lunch hall duty. She also ran two drama clubs and organised the school magazine. Northwold was slave labour. They squeezed every last drop from each person in the name of economy. They didn't even pay the going rate. Orla felt she had no more drops to give. She had sixty books to mark but no desire to do so. There was something about dealing with children that drained her of her energy. They demanded of her constantly, required her to sort out their endless squabbling and bullying incidents, help them with every aspect of their lives. By the time she arrived home in the evening, there was no time to try to build a social life or have hobbies. She had no energy left to deal with people. She envied those who had little jobs, those who could come home and please themselves about what they did in the evening, untrammelled by marking and planning and the constant nagging worries over progress and examination results. How lovely that must be!

She knew she was unravelling. Her enthusiasm had ebbed away, little by little; with each slight and defeat, her spirit had contracted. She had tried to tell herself that the boys made up for it. At first they had. There were moments. She had taught them to love poetry. They brought her their efforts—dropped them on her desk secretly, like rare jewels. She shared their triumphs and disasters, matches won and lost. She searched for books they would like, often buying them herself, nurturing a love of the written word. There were some successes, many failures. It wasn't enough for her anymore. She had lost herself somewhere, mislaid her compass. Orla was trapped...a spider in amber.

She needed to make a change.

Orla closed her eyes and leaned back in the soft chair. She lived entirely alone, save for her tabby cat, Grimalkin, who could not be said to actually live there. He came in for food and went out again. He was a poor companion. Orla had few friends, virtually by choice. She had tried at first, invited people from school to dinner, attended dull drinks parties and interminable classical concerts. She soon realised she had nothing in common with the staff. They seemed to yearn for the world to be permanently 1925—or possibly 1825. Some of them had made catty comments about her taste in paintings, lampshades, furniture...whatever. Orla found them ridiculous, tweedy, dull, dead. The tiny village in which she lived offered few social opportunities. She had no wish to go to slimming classes in the draughty hall or learn to play bridge with her elderly neighbours. The church was not of her faith. She had given up and retreated into herself. Orla tried to think of what she should do. Nothing came to her mind. She had no money. The cottage was rented. She had never saved for a deposit to buy anything. She was a spendthrift, spending her meagre wages on things she couldn't afford: killer heels she rarely wore, lingerie no man would ever see, organic food, expensive red wine, hardback books, luxury bedding. At the end of each month, her bank account appeared to be in arrears without her having noticed. Escape seemed impossible. Orla's mind formed a picture of a forlorn weed struggling to survive in a featureless, brown desert.

She shook her head, desperate to banish the gloom. It was dangerous to think these thoughts. They would overtake her, sink her. Orla cast about for something more pleasant. Elijah's face swam into her mind. She smiled and allowed herself to dwell on him for some delicious moments. Here were more dangerous thoughts, but of a more cheerful kind. As she summoned his image, a warm glow seemed to envelop her, starting from her stomach and spreading outwards, down to the tips of her toes and stretching to her fingers. The unaccustomed feeling was delightful. She basked in it, stretching herself out like a lazy cat on a hot roof terrace. Orla's mind was swamped in yellow sunshine. She felt herself grow hot between her legs. She mouthed his name in a silent prayer and felt herself drifting to sleep. Orla dreamed she was flying across empty prairies and along long, winding rivers towards some unknown ocean.

She was flying somewhere, somewhere better…

CHAPTER FOUR

The term settled itself into its usual dull, deadening routine. Orla buried her strange feelings deep inside her and locked them away. She felt no real guilt about them but knew she was supposed to. The sisters at her Roman Catholic school had taught her that lust was wrong a long time ago. Sex was only for making babies. Love was somehow allowed. Catholic girls' sex education had consisted of telling the girls that they would get married and their husbands would love them. How they would love them had never actually been mentioned. The girls had been left in a haze of ignorance. They had gleaned their knowledge from gossip and magazines, television programmes that cut away at the crucial moment, apocryphal tales from girls who had gone all the way with their older boyfriends, scary stories of pain and blood. In Orla's house, sex had been a forbidden topic. The repressive atmosphere of a Catholic Scottish education did not make for healthy adults. Orla was a lapsed Catholic, or thought she was. She couldn't quite escape it. She still believed in God, very strongly, but she had stopped observing the rituals. She hadn't stepped inside the Catholic church in the nearest town for years. Intellectually, she had rejected the church. Her mind examined the position of women, the rules on contraception, the child abuse scandals, and threw it out. There was so much that was not right. And yet it gnawed away at her. She loved the Bible, the beauty of the King James version, the exquisite poetry of the psalms. Orla felt instinctively that the teachings of the church on the subject of sex were just evil. To deny natural feelings, to make them guilt ridden, could only lead to trouble. The river of lust, denied its natural channels, would come out in other twisted, polluted waterways.

Was it lust she had felt for Elijah?

She wasn't quite certain. Something. Not quite lust. Love at first sight? What was love? She had read enough about it in English literature, but she was none the wiser. Orla tried to analyse her feelings, but she couldn't fathom them. Every time she saw Elijah, she felt elated, like a great joy was welling up inside her. Her body wanted to reach out to touch him, to hold him as if this was the most natural thing, and yet it wasn't just physical. Their conversation was so easy; it was as if they already knew each other's thoughts. She enjoyed just being near him. Nobody had ever had this much effect on Orla, and yet it was impossible to act upon. If there was a method in the universe, as Orla still believed, then why had he been sent to her? Perhaps he was a trial to test her. So she must resist her feelings. Orla wished she could stop being good, wished that she could give in to her instincts, be bad with abandonment. In her youth, she had longed for a grand passion, but it had never happened. Men had proven to be a disappointment to her. Their interest in her had usually been physical. She had never managed to meet anyone she could really talk to, no one who actually wanted to be with her and listen to her ideas. She had wanted to talk about poetry and art, but the engineers and vets of Edinburgh University had other ideas. She remembered their hot hands and beer breath as they pushed themselves against her in subterranean nightclubs.

Love was very different from what she had read about in Victorian novels and Tudor poetry. It was not refined. It was animal. And yet in spite of the way she had walled herself up in the school, in the countryside, she had still somehow kept a little hope burning that one day love would find her. Elijah seemed to have made the little flame burn brighter. Orla couldn't allow herself to think like this. He was underage, still a child. She was trusted to teach him, to look after him. She must be professional. So she placed her heart in a wooden chest and padlocked it shut, deliberately mislaying the key.

It wasn't as if she hadn't had relationships, but somehow they had all failed. At fifteen, she had been raped by a sixth-form boy in her school boiler room. It was something she never allowed herself to think about. It hadn't even been rape but sexual assault, as he had not been able to perform the act. Orla had told nobody. As a result of this unfortunate experience, she had ducked out of the usual teenage romances. At university, she had spent first year enduring a series of one-night stands with men she was too drunk to brush off and avoiding the advances of some less favoured individuals whom she had no interest in. She had finally managed a relationship with Christopher, a well-scrubbed boy from the Home Counties. She'd tried to kid herself that she loved him, but she hadn't. He had had at least some good qualities. He was tall and quite good looking, with some charm and an ease of manner, which won him friends. But ultimately there was a shallowness in him that meant there was really nothing to love. Orla had liked the idea of a boyfriend. It made her feel normal, as if she was as other people were. But she wasn't. He dumped her unceremoniously in the second year with a short letter sent to her home in the long vacation. Then he told all his friends she was frigid. So that was that. Orla had no idea what she had done wrong. They'd had sex regularly. It was unremarkable. She didn't feel very much. He had made no attempt to give her pleasure. It had all been about him.

She hadn't satisfied him. She didn't know how. She had been completely sheltered and knew nothing of such things. Maybe he was right. She wondered if it was because she didn't love him enough. He certainly hadn't loved her. He had just liked the idea of a pretty girl on his arm.

Vacuous.

Empty.

Then there had been Oriel. Not an undergraduate, he was a Jamaican by birth, black as cinders. He sold drugs to the students and lived in a flashy flat in Stockbridge full of modern art and uncomfortable, old, tatty furniture that was apparently trendy. People referred to it as nouveau-squat. She had moved in with him on the second date. They got married in a registry office after six months, under the influence of LSD, with two dazed tramps from the street as witnesses. That was Oriel.

Crazy.

As crazy as Orla.

They had had a kind of painful, twisted love. Well, Orla thought she had loved him. Oriel was incapable of love. He was in lust with her, perhaps. She still hadn't managed her meeting of minds. It was more like a meeting of bodies. He was achingly beautiful to her. She loved making love to him, the smell of him, the smoothness of his skin, the way he made her forget everything else. So she learned about sex and how to give and receive pleasure. It was so easy with him. She had hoped it would be enough, but somehow it wasn't. She still felt the emptiness. Her soul was searching, still, for someone to share itself with, but that person was nowhere to be found. Oriel did not have very much to say. He was interested in football, marijuana, and music. He was not interested in books. Orla had not found a soulmate in him. She just allowed things to happen to her. He took the lead and she followed. She knew in her heart it was only physical love, the lowest form. Yet she enjoyed the physical love, needed it.

She spent her time studying in the library, listening in tutorials to tortuous arguments in which she rarely ventured a view, lying stoned on the sofa in Oriel's flat, listening to music designed for this purpose...music to make you feel in a trance. Indeed, her whole life seemed to be a trance, a dream in which she watched herself with little interest.

Shortly after Orla's graduation, the police raided the flat looking for drugs, and Oriel was deported back to Jamaica. She still had vivid dreams about that morning: waking in the coldness of the dawn light to the sound of the battering ram at the door, the explosion of uniformed men who hurtled into the bedroom. They had ignored Orla. It was Oriel they wanted. She was just a woman, and they had no curiosity about her. Oriel had submitted to them without a fight, totally calm. It had surprised her. He was fixed in her mind like a Christian martyr accepting his fate from those who didn't understand him. To Orla he had done nothing wrong. He was not a heroin dealer, nothing bad or dirty. He sold grass and LSD. He made people feel good. He let them find escape from the humdrum reality they found themselves in. How was this wrong? The world seemed run by people who wanted to deny pleasure from other people—hard, miserable people. She divorced him and trained as a teacher due to her failure to find any gainful employment in Edinburgh. She had not stood by her man.

There had been no boyfriends to speak of since Oriel.

Elijah and Orla became friends. Of course they weren't supposed to be friends. She was meant to maintain professional distance, as it was known in the trade. And yet she couldn't. It didn't seem to matter to her or to him that she was a teacher and he was a pupil. They just got on. She found him a pleasurable companion. He became one of her projects, like Rupert. There seemed to be an immediate bond between them, like a ribbon that invisibly snaked across the ether, binding them to each other. She could always tell when he was in a room. She always knew what he was thinking. They finished each other's sentences. He entered her dreams often and seemed permanently to have taken up residence in the background of her mind.

Orla managed to negotiate the labyrinthine ways of the school's Admissions Department to finally locate Elijah's paperwork. It had taken some terse emails and rude phone calls. The secretaries liked to guard their territory like Rottweilers, behaving as if they were protecting state secrets for MI6. She perused his American school report cards to try to discover why he had been placed two years behind. He had been to six different schools. His father was some bigwig in the US Air Force. His mother had died when he was eight. As far as she could see, there had been no counselling. He was of slightly above average IQ, with a reading age of sixteen, but his writing was like that of a five-year-old. He printed and did not join, spidering his writing across the page and paying no attention to the lines. His spelling was appalling. Orla read, "Elijah is orally excellent," in the neat hand of one of his teachers. It was true. He could talk, confidently debating points with her that were lost on the others. He could empathise with characters and discuss nuances of feeling. Orally excellent. He was a conundrum. She didn't get him. There was more. She found some guarded allusions to behavioural problems. There had been two suspensions for fighting. More disturbingly, there was a photograph of what she presumed to be Elijah's back, showing dark bruises, red weals, and small circular marks. Were they cigarette burns? There was nothing on the back, no attached notes, no explanation. It was just tucked in between a pile of reports. Orla tucked it back and returned the papers to admissions.

Perhaps it was there by mistake, she told herself.

Orla phoned his father, who stated that the only problem Elijah had was laziness. He needed firm discipline. He seemed far away, uninterested. Orla felt he saw her as a woolly liberal who was not capable of managing Elijah. Probably he was right. Discipline was not Orla's strong point. The father was cold. *He probably believes in bringing back hanging and flogging,* Orla thought as she put the phone down.

She was no further forward.

But Orla slowly wove her magic on Elijah, wrapping him in her educational spell. He had stated firmly that he didn't like reading. She delved into the library and tried out various excerpts on him, evincing his interests to find a match. Eventually she cracked him with spy novels, young James Bonds, Flashman, war stories of derring-do—male and violent. He began to read for pleasure. The writing was harder. He held the pen like a sword, stabbing in frustration at the page. She wondered if he had been naturally left-handed and forced to change. It was rare these days, but it still happened. Orla coaxed him to change his grip, checked him at two-minute intervals.

"Pen! Pen!" was all she had to bark at him in the end, and he would smile and do as she asked.

She taught him to join from ancient handwriting textbooks she found in the attic store cupboard above her room. He stayed behind on Tuesdays and Thursdays, copying out Victorian poems and worthy epigrams in newfound swirls. She arranged spelling lessons for him with the starchy learning support teacher, who reported him as lazy, rude, and disruptive.

"Disruptive? On his own in a private lesson?" Orla inquired, exasperated.

She had never found him so. In fact, he was easy, keen to learn, wanting to please.

Orla did not yet realise he only did this for her.

So far, so professional. Orla thought she had conquered her strange feelings. She worked and worked, so she didn't have to think, didn't have to feel. She lived for others.

There was no Orla.

CHAPTER FIVE

Elijah had his own ideas. Unprofessional ideas.
Elijah fitted well into Northwold life. He was adaptable. He grew out his hair like everybody else. He learned to play rugby and was soon in the A team. He had an easy charm, which he switched on to people who mattered to him: Orla, the tuck shop lady, the rugby coach. With others he couldn't be bothered. He was indifferent to them, almost contemptuous. Elijah did enough work to get by—no more, no less. He was not unpopular, but he had no close friends. It was as if he didn't really need people. In spite of his unfamiliar name and accent, he was never bullied. The other boys seemed slightly afraid of him. In spite of the fact that the American airbase was less than ten miles away, he was a full boarder and never went home for weekends like so many of the others. This was the only thing he had in common with little Rupert.

The boarders were mostly a forlorn little bunch. They stuck closely to each other, huddling together as if a bitter wind was blowing them over. They formed intense little friendships, coupled and uncoupled through the term. Some of them were as young as seven. Many wet the bed and cried themselves to sleep every night. This was the reason Orla had refused to live in the school in spite of intense pressure to do so. She would not have been able to stand it. The matron was brisk and no-nonsense: stop all this fuss, pull yourself together, stiff upper lip, be a man, play up, play up, and play the game.

What rot! thought Orla.

Why was it so important to learn not to feel? What were the boys being prepared for? The British Empire was long dead. Were Victorian values going to do them any good in the modern age? Orla didn't think so. She sometimes wondered how many of them would die before her in American wars, fall in desert lands far away, fighting for something nobody understood.

On Sundays, they had brunch at ten and then had to survive until six for supper. They complained of hunger constantly. Orla gave them forbidden biscuits and sweets, padlocked up by the matron. Elijah had found the key for her. She was on duty every other weekend now, as others cried off with family commitments. Orla had no family commitments. Her longing for a child of her own had receded to a dull ache, which she had become so accustomed to that she barely noticed it any more. She took them in the minibus on listless outings to places in which they had no interest. They wanted to go home like other boys and play violent computer games and watch rap videos. They did not want this regimented life. Orla always felt slightly mortified by their behaviour whenever they went out. They marched along pavements, three abreast, refusing to give way to elderly ladies and mothers with pushchairs. They asked the monks in Norwich Cathedral how much they earned. They complained loudly how boring everything was in the East Anglian Railway Museum and refused to sit down in the little train, causing the red-faced guard to explode in rage. It was all, of course, Orla's fault.

Everything was Orla's fault.

"Don't you mind boarding?" Orla asked Elijah one evening.

They were huddled in her classroom going over his January examination paper. He had received the lowest mark in the year, much to Orla's annoyance.

"No, I don't get homesick. I am used to it," he replied.

Nothing bothered him.

Orla tried to speak to him severely, but she never quite managed it. Before long, he had deftly switched the conversation from the paper to Orla. She found herself telling him about her childhood in the old grey house in Peterhead. Her family had originally made money from Arctic whaling but was long since gone. Her grandfather had given her the horn of a narwhal, telling her he cut it from a dead unicorn, and she had run round the garden with it, casting spells on the flowers. Orla roused herself from her nostalgia, noting that it was already twenty to six.

"Come on, Elijah, we *must* get on. It's nearly suppertime. 'Ozymandias.' Question 3: What effect do the words 'two vast and trunkless legs of stone' have on the stanza? What have you written? 'These words are effective because they have a great effect and Miss McKenzie loves this poem, so it must be good.'"

Orla collapsed into giggles at the ridiculousness of the answer. She laid her head down on the desk, giving herself up to her laughter.

"That's the worst answer I have ever read in my entire career," Orla lied.

Elijah appeared unconcerned at his lack of prowess in literary criticism and helped himself to a piece of coffee cake, which Orla had purloined from the staff common room.

"Find the words in the poem and highlight them. Step one," Orla ordered in what she hoped was her most commanding voice.

Elijah swallowed the cake whole and ran his fingers along the lines of the poem without interest.

"I can't find them," he whined plaintively.

"There."

"Where?"

"There."

Orla put her finger on the correct line, which was perilously close to his finger. He put his hand over hers and rested it there. In shock, she allowed this to go on for rather too many seconds and then took her hand away.

"Stop it!" she hissed fiercely.

He seemed unperturbed. They carried on working through the poem for another ten minutes, and then she let him go to supper. On leaving she told him how hard he had worked, how pleased she was with him, and how much progress he had made. She did not mean any of it but had gone into professional autopilot.

So it started—in small ways, almost imperceptibly.

The snow stayed for a few weeks and then suddenly receded. The wind stayed bitter, but snowdrops appeared overnight in little drifts under the trees where Frank had carefully planted them, defiantly heralding the longed-for spring. Orla decided on a new health kick and took up jogging after school. It was dark by the time she could go, so she took a little torch with her. Elijah decided it was too dark for her on her own and announced his intention to go with her.

"You can't," Orla said flatly.

"Why?"

"You just can't."

"Why?"

"It would be weird."

"Why?"

She gave in.

They went jogging together every weekday evening. He was much faster than her of course. Sometimes he ran on ahead and waited for her in little clearings under the trees.

"Don't laugh at me," she would say.

"I am not," he would reply and then continue to laugh.

They would arrive, hot and breathless, late for supper, and would sit together at the long wooden tables and eat whatever leftovers were available. The food was generally awful, high on carbohydrate, low on anything expensive. One particular evening, Elijah was having pasta, potato salad, and chips.

"Yeugh! Have some stodge with your stodge why don't you?" Orla laughed.

Orla was having salad and potatoes. Elijah took revenge.

"You shouldn't be eating potatoes. They make you fat. You said you were on a diet."

"You are having them!"

"Yes, but I'm not fat."

Orla took her fork and stabbed him in the hand with it, not with any force. The housemaster walked by and coughed theatrically. Orla withdrew her fork and looked down at the plate, annoyed that they had attracted attention.

They talked easily to each other about everything and anything, sometimes joking, sometimes serious. It was as if the rest of the world would melt away into soft focus and there were only Elijah and Orla left. Often, Orla would become aware that everyone else had gone and they were alone in the dining room save for the kitchen staff, sweeping up around them, irritated but too timid to ask them to leave. Orla would rouse herself with a start, like a fallow deer lit up by car headlights on a dark country road, amazed at how quickly the time went whenever he was there, and rush off to her next task.

Surprisingly to Orla, their intense friendship seemed to cause little stir among the staff. It was not usually commented upon. Many of the boys had had crushes on her in the past; they still did. Orla put it down to a heady mix of hormones and desperation. She didn't take them seriously, laughing off their clumsy compliments and awkward flirtations. Fraser was a particular example.

He would call her "baby," tell her she looked hot in her outfits, say to his friends rather too loudly that she was a MILF and he would like to do her. Orla enjoyed the ebb and flow of their conversations, but both parties knew there was nothing in it. It was just meaningless fun. She knew she should be more severe with Fraser, but she was usually laughing too much to manage it. Somehow Elijah made her feel different. She could not explain it. He had never said anything crude to her.

The friendship between Orla and Elijah strengthened and grew as the term rumbled on, and as it did so, her relations with others diminished. Somewhere in her mind a small voice warned her that trouble would come of it, but Orla had been too long in the desert to listen to it. He was like a well she had found in the midst of her lonely journey, and she had stopped to drink, luxuriating in the cool, fresh water, pouring it over herself, drinking it deeply.

CHAPTER SIX

It was eight o'clock on a Friday evening, and Orla was in the bath. Baths were special to Orla—one of her favourite things. She had them as often as possible. She imagined that in a previous life she must have been Cleopatra, luxuriating in asses' milk poured by half-naked slaves. The bubbles were overflowing onto the wooden floorboards. Orla took a sip of the Rioja, which she had balanced precariously between the taps. She loved red wine. She examined it in the candlelight: liquid rubies. She was trying to teach herself to appreciate wine, so she swirled it round in her mouth. She could taste vanilla definitely, and that was from oak casks. What else? Blackberries maybe. Orla was not very good at telling yet. As she sipped it, the irritations of the day seemed to fall away, and she finally relaxed. The warmth of the water soothed her skin. She had been marinating for about forty minutes, so the pads of her fingers were wrinkled.

Orla finally roused herself, got out, and wrapped herself in a huge white cotton towel. She padded barefoot into the kitchen. She rarely wore shoes in the house, enjoying the feeling of freedom it gave her. Orla's laptop was lying open on the kitchen table. She took a gulp of wine and tapped the machine into life. Orla opened her Facebook page. She had been a member for about two years, but after the initial novelty she'd got bored of looking at other people's baby photos, holidays, and apparently perfect lives. The smiling faces just fed into her ever-growing sense of inadequacy. Somewhere inside she knew that this was just a façade that people erected against the world. Their lives probably contained many hidden, unsavoury secrets, but the effect of the profiles still bothered Orla. Her interest had been reawakened recently by Nathaniel, an old university friend who had found her page and befriended her. Orla had been amazed that he had remembered her and looked for her name. He was a corporate lawyer in London, married to another corporate lawyer. He had a flat in Canary Wharf, a Jaguar E-type, and a Persian cat called Estella. Orla clicked on his pictures and admired his photos for the fifth time that week. There were work bashes where he was standing in black tie, holding a champagne glass, surrounded by glamorous women in long dresses, exotic holidays in the Caribbean and the United States, family gatherings with lots of elderly ladies in appalling hats. He appeared to have the perfect middle-class existence. However, it had not escaped Orla's notice that there were no children. This seemed the only smudge on the burnished steel of Nathaniel's life. He was still incredibly good looking. He was tall, six foot five at least, with curling blond hair, an easy smile showing surprisingly crooked teeth, and a broad chest. He was like a big, woolly polar bear whom Orla just longed to cuddle and be cradled in his huge hands. Orla and Nathaniel had been conducting a rather bizarre online affair for about two months. They hadn't actually met, but Orla kind of hoped he was building up to it slowly. He was married, but if she was truthful, she felt no guilt. After all, he had started it.

The online conversations were mostly about sex. He had started out quite nervously and then gained confidence. They made up little scenarios and had conversations with each other in character. Sometimes he was a Roman soldier coming home on leave to his wife, sometimes he was a political leader visiting his mistress in a bijou city apartment, sometimes he was a Japanese samurai paying a visit to a geisha house. Orla loved these conversations and looked forward to them daily. The geisha scenario was Orla's favourite. She wanted very much to be a geisha. She felt so comfortable with the idea of a woman made for pleasure, whose every elegant gesture and movement was taught to entice and charm. Orla wished that she and Nathaniel could really live in this imaginary bubble they had created. The sex they had in these situations was perfect: passionate and yet tender and loving. Truly, Orla thought she had found the perfect man—a man who understood her needs as she understood his. Nathaniel was erudite and educated. Orla hoped they would one day be able to converse about books and poetry as easily as they talked about sex.

She hoped.

This was, in fact, the nearest Orla had had to a relationship for over a decade. She was pretty fussy, she supposed, and nobody in her rural Suffolk surroundings had ever pricked her interest. She wondered if she set too much store on looks, but she knew she couldn't contemplate a relationship with anyone who didn't excite her physically. None of the teachers ever had. Some of the fathers were almost passable, the almost dashing Royal Air Force officers, but of course they were all married, and most were not really her type, to say the least. Nathaniel did excite her physically. It was not lost on her that he was of a similar type to Elijah and probably looked like Elijah would in the future. Nathaniel was perfect, bodily at least.

Orla clicked on to Nathaniel's wedding album and regarded his wife critically. She was tall, maybe about six feet, with long auburn hair, which Orla presumed was dyed. It was too shiny and rich to be a real colour. Orla couldn't decide if she was facially plain or not. She was not very good at telling with women. She was no great beauty, that was for sure. Her features were broad and flat, giving the impression more of a strapping farm girl than a lawyer. Her large shoulders would mean she could heft hay bales around with ease. She had a strong jaw, which made Orla feel she wouldn't like to cross her; there was a sense of self-confidence bordering on aggression. Her eyes were brown and seemed to stare ferociously into the camera. She was always very heavily made up, even in casual snaps. Orla wondered if this betrayed an insecurity about her looks. Even in her wedding dress, she looked slightly overweight; her stomach protruded through the fabric. Orla knew her thoughts were becoming unkind, but she could not seem to help it. The wedding looked perfect, the kind of affair they photographed in wedding magazines, very different from Orla's register office affair with Oriel. Nathaniel's wife was wearing a simple, plain white dress with a bouquet of perfect lilies. There were three blond, tiny bridesmaids with rosebuds in their hair. The church looked old, ancient even, with mossy gravestones in front. Nathaniel looked stunning in a morning suit. It was the sort of wedding Orla had dreamed of as child, but somehow she had known even then that it wasn't likely to happen. She had kind of always thought the riches required to pay for such an occasion would never be hers. Orla wondered what Nathaniel saw in his wife, telling herself that she was probably very sweet and kind. Hmmm. Maybe. From the look of her, Orla knew that this just didn't seem likely. Perhaps it was her success and relative wealth. She was bound to come from a good family: the "real thing" no doubt, as the snobs of Northwold would say. They suited each other—the perfect couple. Yet not so perfect: Nathaniel was playing away.

Orla looked down at the chat box, but Nathaniel was not online. She was disappointed. She could have done with the lift of some flirtatious conversation. She was just in the mood. Of course he was not online—it was Friday evening. He would be out at some glamorous event. Only Orla was in alone. Well, not quite; there must be other sad spinsters. She thought of them sitting in their rooms all over England. She wondered how they coped with it, what lies they told themselves. They had all fallen into the feminist trap. Get a job. Be independent. Don't rely on a man. Have a glorious career. This was the message to the modern woman that screamed from the metropolitan magazines, which Orla had stopped reading long ago. Yet as these women approached midlife, they realised they had not much to show for themselves. They were alone with careers that had never quite taken off as they hoped. Men seemed to favour other men. They promoted each other, and the women were left in more lowly roles…just as they had always been. Of course, a few had broken through: one even becoming prime minister. Yet they seemed the exception rather than the rule. Orla had stayed on the bottom rung. She sometimes thought there must be something wrong with her, but she suspected it was because she was a woman, and a quite pretty one at that. She was supposed to get married and have children, not have a serious career. Nathaniel's wife was successful, of course. This bothered Orla. That was the sort of woman he went for, and Orla could not compete with that. She must have behaved like a man to get on, elbowed others out of the way, been self-confident, ruthless, focussed—everything that Orla was not. She felt, when she thought of this, a failure. She had failed at work and failed in her personal life. She was a freak, a weirdo, a misfit…such thoughts were running in Orla's head more and more these days. She filled herself with work to keep the thoughts at bay. She felt normal when she was with Elijah—she felt special, that she was worth something…a friend. He made her feel attractive, wanted, full of life, interesting. But he was too young. It was not allowed. Fate was cruel to her: giving her something and then making it impossible.

Orla clicked back to her own page and saw that she had two new friend requests. One was from Fraser, her child admirer from school. Again. He tried to be her friend about once a month. She pressed ignore and looked at the other one. It was, amazingly, from Oriel. She hesitated. Here was surely trouble. Curiosity got the better of her, and she clicked the Add button. His page had obviously only recently been set up. He had one photo and only seven friends. The information was minimal. She could tell little about his life other than that his location was Jamaica and he was working as a "businessman." There was no sign of a wife. Orla wondered about him for several minutes and what had happened to him in the intervening years.

Orla left the screen on and went back to her wine. She read her novel for a while, dozed, and then attempted some television. She clicked through a dozen channels, watching each offering for about two minutes before dismissing it. There was nothing she liked these days. She was endlessly horrified by the footage of relentless wars, famines, and natural disasters, but she felt helpless to do anything. She wasn't interested in the family Friday night fare of light entertainment. She supposed she had quite serious taste. She loved European cinema, Shakespeare plays, and old jazz. Not much was available in rural Suffolk. Orla daydreamed of living in Paris, shuffling around dimly lit cafes, smoking and drinking cognac, having earnest arguments with writers and artists. That was life! She had a framed photograph of Samuel Beckett doing just this: sitting in a Paris cafe smoking a cigarette, staring without expression into the camera. His face was so lined he appeared as old as a person could ever be. Orla admired the work of Beckett greatly. She wanted to be in the cafe with him, talking to him earnestly, admiring him, nurturing him. But she had never met anyone like this. Great writers did not frequent cafes and bars in obscure Suffolk villages. In fact, there were no cafes and bars to frequent.

Orla returned to the computer, checked again if Nathaniel was online, and found that he wasn't. She felt irritated with herself for becoming obsessive about it. He would probably come in drunk about two in the morning and send her a message promising to do something vaguely disgusting to her in the near future. Orla sighed and downed the rest of the wine. She had now drunk the whole bottle and was slightly woozy.

Then it happened.

A friend request appeared from Elijah Haynes with a message: "Good evening Miss McKenzie. I hope you are having a pleasant weekend. Xxx."

Orla smiled to herself at the formality of the note, not like his usual style. Her finger hovered over the Ignore button, but she did not press it. She sat motionless for some minutes. Then the devil came into her, not for the first time, and she clicked Add. Orla immediately clicked onto his page. He had 562 friends, mostly teenagers from what she could see, and about twenty photo albums. Orla spent a pleasant half an hour looking at endless pictures of family holidays. Elijah got slightly taller in each album. There were none of anyone who could possibly be his mother. Orla was disappointed in this, as she was intrigued to see what she had looked like.

A green circle appeared next to the name Elijah Haynes in the chat box.

He was online.

Orla glanced at the kitchen clock: eleven thirty. He should be asleep. A message appeared in the corner of the screen:

"Hello Miss McKenzie ☺"

Orla hesitated. A minute ticked by. She felt herself grow hot and felt her sweat seeping into the towel. She knew she should ignore it. She didn't.

"Hello, Elijah. Why aren't you in bed?"

"I am in bed. I am on my iPhone under the covers. Nobody can see me."

"How are you on Facebook?"

"It's an app on the phone, stupid. ☺ ☺ ☺"

"Go to sleep."

"No I'm not sleepy. How is my favourite baby?"

"Don't call me baby."

"Why?"

"I don't know. It's disrespectful."

"No it isn't. It's nice. Baby. X"

"You shouldn't be talking to me."

"Why? It's fun. xxx"

"You are so naughty."

"That's me. Naughty boy. That's why you like me."

"I'm drunk. I can't trust myself to be sensible."

"Woohoo. You are an alcoholic. Don't be sensible. Who wants to be sensible?"

"OK."

A minute of silence elapsed, and Orla thought he had gone. Then…

"I love you Miss McKenzie ☺ ☺ ☺ ☺ ☺"

"I love you too, Elijah. Because you make me laugh."

Orla was shocked at herself. She closed the screen and shut the computer. She had enjoyed the interaction, feeling his warmth and humour emanating from the cold, hard screen. Was it wrong? She didn't really feel any guilt. What was it they always said at school? Inappropriate. Anything fun was inappropriate. Part of her didn't care. Part of her did. Orla resolved not to do it again.

She returned to her book and ploughed through a few more chapters, trying to block Elijah from her mind. He kept creeping back there, unbidden, like a burglar with stealthy, silent footsteps. Orla sighed. She returned to the laptop and flipped it open. On opening Facebook, she found a message from Nathaniel: "I want to kiss your labia."

Orla sighed. She felt the contrast with the conversation with Elijah. He spoke of love. Nathaniel spoke of lust. The boy. The man. She wished Nathaniel would see her in something other than sexual terms, but that didn't seem likely to happen any time soon. Perhaps she should start an opening gambit about philosophy or modern art.

Stupidly, Orla wrote, "I love you Nathaniel. Xxx."

Orla was not certain if this was true or not. She was not certain what love was anymore. She loved Elijah. She knew it, but it was impossible. She wanted to love Nathaniel. Love, or something like it, had been building up to hurricane force in her for years. Now it was ready to burst the levees and force its way through and out. Unstoppable, irresistible. Nathaniel would have to be the recipient.

Orla opened a file on her laptop marked "Love." In it, she had kept copies of all the Facebook conversations with Nathaniel. She had them all, neatly ordered into subfiles. She clicked on the file marked "Geisha" and allowed herself to luxuriate in the previously held conversation. She read the words aloud, using different voices for Nathaniel's character and her own. She was an older geisha in feudal Japan. She was in charge of the House of the Women, a place of pleasure for the men, in fact a kind of upmarket brothel. He was a soldier, back from another war.

> Orla: The geisha can see the lord has had an American education. He does not understand the exquisite pain of deferred pleasure. The subtle arts of the East may be wasted on him. She does not expect love in the way he understands it. She has no use for marriage as she has her own power. She has a wealthy patron who desires of her no more than

an ornament. The lord is like a young, impetuous boy, but his years suggest he has spent too long on the plains of the West and he has not gained a great deal in wisdom. She has much to teach him. However, she has great affection for the lord, so she takes pity on him and unbars the heavy gate.

Nathaniel: The lord is dust-caked and weary, fresh from battle. He is thirsty for nectar, hungry for sweet oblivion. He bangs his fist on the door of the House of Women. He does not know the workings of his heart. His intentions are now. He wants to be held, his shaking body fixed in the present.

He reaches out to touch her.

Orla: He unties her kimono and it drops to reveal her shoulders and her large, firm breasts. Her skin is so white like a statue.

Nathaniel: He has so often dreamt of this moment, it sustained him in the wilderness.

Orla: She is not supposed to give herself to him by tradition. She belongs to the patron. But there are no other men in the House of the Women. She will do as she pleases. She finds him so alluring. She leads him to the bed, which is raised on a platform in the centre of the chamber.

Nathaniel: She is exactly the same as she ever was, timeless, a haven of peace in the midst of the storm.

Orla: She smiles up at him. She is not a girl. She has known many men. She has lain with his father, who despairs of him. She knows all of the secrets of the men. She does not tell. She knows he is a good man, but he has not tamed his passions. He has not gone into the stillness. She understands this. She is patient. She kisses his forehead gently and thinks of the first time he came to her long ago when he was very young. He has not changed so very much.

Nathaniel: He is so grateful to her.

Orla: So he feels he has waited for eternity. She comes in eventually and serves him tea. He watches her intently. He can see the perfectly white nape of her neck and a hint of her breasts through the folds of the kimono. She asks him to tell her of the war far away. He does so with weariness. He is tired of war. He drinks the tea, which is bitter but fragrant. She kneels close to him.

Nathaniel: Go on. Is he carried to the bed?

Orla: Always the rush. NO. The virgins dress him and they brush his hair. They spray him with perfume. They oil his chafed skin with ointment. They lead him to her chamber, where he sits on a chair and waits. First he has to be bathed. She won't do it as her status is too high. The girls of the house cover him in soap. They giggle when they see his manhood, as they are still innocent. They wash him in the bath. He feels sleepy.

Nathaniel: He gives himself up to her completely.

Orla: The geisha is moved by his unaccustomed humility. The matrons of the house carry him to the bathhouse. The water is heated.

Nathaniel: He throws off his weapons and his dusty clothes and he falls to his knees before her, a supplicant…

Orla: The geisha has been trained since childhood to give sensual pleasure. The flower does not open easily. It needs much preparation and gentle coaxing. The eroticism is in the promise of what may be given, or may not. That depends upon the lord being pure in heart and intention. It is not easy to gain access to the House of the Women, but once he has found the key, the rewards are sweet as honey.

Nathaniel: He wants her very much. He imagines her parting the leaves of her kimono…unfurled flower a bead of dew on the petal nectar.

Orla stopped reading, and her eyes filled with tears. She wanted this scenario so much, desperately wanted it to be real, wanted to give all her love to Nathaniel, her body and her mind.

She could not love Elijah.

"You do not love Elijah. You can't," Orla spoke aloud.

She hadn't convinced herself.

CHAPTER SEVEN

The next day was Saturday. It dawned cold but bright and clear. Orla woke at dawn, groaned, turned over, felt her head thumping, and went back to sleep. The bedroom was ice cold, so Orla bundled herself inside the duvet so that no part of her was visible. She slept fitfully through the morning, dreaming alternately of Nathaniel and Elijah. In her waking minutes, she had a particularly vivid daydream concerning Nathaniel.

They lived together in a little house in a small village in Kent; Orla had successfully persuaded him to move out of the city. Of course, the wife was a distant memory. Nathaniel went to work on the train, and Orla kept the house and wrote romantic novels in the afternoons. They had three children: identical male triplets. Their life together was idyllic. They adored each other, and their children were clever and sporty. The house was small but cosy and filled with antiques from exotic lands, which Nathaniel had inherited from his parents. In the dream, it was always sunny and a yellow glow covered everything. The garden was filled with flowers. It wasn't so very difficult, this dream. It was no more than what many people had—well, apart from the triplets. Yet Orla knew it was not possible. She had given up hope of these things long ago. Nathaniel's interest in her was purely sexual. He wanted to fuck her, as he had stated plainly one evening last week. Charm itself! Beyond that, he had no plans. It was true she wanted to fuck him back. Her logical mind knew it was a sexual infatuation. Her soul hoped for something more, though, so much more. She had longed all her life for a grand romance: a meeting of bodies but also of minds, a sharing of ideas and values, a shared life. It had never happened. Maybe she had filled herself up with nonsense when she was a girl, read too many silly books, watched too many silly films, filling her heart with romantic ideas. She couldn't seem to escape the longing, the feeling of emptiness, the sense that out there somewhere was a person who could make her feel whole, complete.

It had never happened.

So Orla spent time in daydreams, as reality seemed to offer little comfort to her bruised soul. But in spite of her telling herself it was out of the question, a tiny seed of hope planted itself inside her and tried to germinate itself. Maybe it wasn't a daydream. Maybe it was a premonition. On occasion, she had dreamed the future—rarely. "Don't be stupid!" she said to herself angrily. Things like that didn't happen to Orla. They only seemed to happen to other people. Still, the seed stirred and forced out a root, probing for sustenance deep inside Orla.

In her sleeping moments, she dreamed of Elijah. There was nothing concrete—just his face swimming into focus against a blurred background and the feeling that always went with him of warmth and light. He was always smiling in the dreams, smiling at Orla, looking right into her, penetrating her with his eyes. There were voices calling her name.

Orla,
Orla,
ORLA.

Not Elijah's voice, other voices—ghostly and distant at first, then louder and insistent, nearer. Orla woke with a start and shook the voices out of her head. This happened to her a lot, and she did not like it. She had always been what her grandmother had called *sensitive*. She could sense things. She knew things without being told. Orla had felt the spirits around her from an early age. She had talked to them, and they had talked to her. They helped her. When she was doing her schoolwork, they had guided her hand, particularly with writing. The pen wrote the words, which flowed without Orla having to do anything—not thinking, not trying, just pouring along across the page, words jumbling out on their own. As she got older, education made the spirits recede. Orla tried to become rational, to be logical, to fit in. But the spirits never quite left. They were just waiting. Now they talked to her at night, in the time before she slept and in the sleeping time. Mostly, she tried to ignore them. She was well aware that voices in the head were considered a sign of madness, of schizophrenia. Deep inside, Orla knew she was not mad; she knew the things she had learned in the worn wooden science labs of her school were not the whole truth—the cold, material world of gas taps, Bunsen burners, and fume cupboards was not the whole story. There was a whole other plane of life, straining through. Orla knew the spirits were real. Sometimes she even caught sight of them, just chinks of them like dawn light through a slatted blind. Some of them were ordinary dead people, probably family members long dead. She didn't recognise them, but there had been few photos in her house. The past was hidden, not much talked about. Some of them seemed different, more exotic, older. She sensed they were from other places, other times. They had chosen to look after Orla, but she didn't know why. What did they want with her? What were they trying to tell her? She didn't know.

She didn't know.

She shook them out of her mind like a girl loosing her hair out of a band after school. She must not listen to them. She didn't want to be special. She didn't want to be different. She wanted to fit in, to be normal. Orla knew she wasn't. People sensed something about her, something they weren't sure of, that they didn't like. They shrank from her. Orla had read about the old times, when a woman of the village would be turned upon, attacked, burned as a witch. She felt empathy with these women. She knew she would have been one of them if she had lived in those times. So she tried clumsily to protect herself from the spirits, not to listen to them. She didn't want to be a martyr like Jeanne d'Arc if that was what they had planned. She wanted ordinary things. In a strange way, she knew that in fact it was the other way round. The spirits were *protecting her.* If something bad was going to happen, she always knew it. She would feel the cold deadness creep up her spine, and she knew trouble was ahead. She was Cassandra. So Orla pretended to be normal. She didn't develop her intuition. She had no guide. She didn't trust the mediums she saw on television and in the paper. They seemed like charlatans and showmen, comforting with talk of banal things that seemed to mean nothing. Orla did not want to be one of them. The church also warned against such things as evil. According to the priests, these beings were not benign dead relatives but demons set on upsetting your life and ruining you. Orla had never felt them so. How could she stand against all these others who knew better? Nobody listened to Orla. So she kept these things quiet, hidden in her dreams. She would not tell.

Orla forced herself to get up, considered having another bath, decided against it, and pulled on her Levi's and a black cashmere sweater. Still barefoot, she padded down to the kitchen and made some scrambled eggs. As it was Saturday, she allowed herself toast with them. Normally, she avoided bread as part of her permanent diet regime. Orla poured herself a black coffee and sat in the armchair next to the Aga, placing her feet on the sheepskin rug, enjoying the feeling of delicious softness between her toes. Unexpectedly her Blackberry phone beeped, and its little angry red light flashed as if sending a signal of alarm. Orla jumped. Hardly anyone ever phoned or texted. She retrieved the phone from the table and read the text message. It was from Nathaniel. "What is up with you? Don't send me ridiculous declarations of love."

Orla could feel his annoyance through the words. She had messed up. She knew she shouldn't have sent him that message last night. Damn the bloody wine. Wine was when the truth came out. Truth was dangerous, not to be spoken.

She replied, "Sorry. I was drunk. Don't be mad."

The reply was immediate. "I am not mad, just surprised. I am coming to see you. I am on the motorway. Are you in?"

Orla was completely shocked. This was not what she had thought was going to happen.

She replied, "What? Yes. OMG."

"I'll be there in an hour. Don't go out. X"

"OK."

Orla put the phone down, still feeling dazed. He couldn't be coming. She was hungover and looked like she had been dragged through a thorny hedge. Orla ran into the bathroom and looked at herself critically in the tiny mirror, the only mirror in the house. As far as she could see, she was not ready to receive an illicit lover. Her hair was sticking up like it had been electrified, and she had dark patches under her eyes. Her eyebrows weren't properly plucked, and her tongue was stained red with the wine. Orla turned the taps in the bath on full. They sputtered and jerked into life.

"Come on!" Orla shouted at them, willing them to pour faster.

She whizzed into the bedroom and opened the pine closet. What was she going to wear? She hadn't seen Nathaniel in person for eighteen years. He was going to think she was fat and old. Orla was not actually overweight at all, but she obsessed about it; it was one of the few things she could control. Black. Black made you look thin. She chose a black woollen sweater dress. She returned to the bathroom and sat on the toilet watching the bath filling. Orla poured in three different smelly concoctions until there were more bubbles than water. It still wasn't full. She breathed in and out slowly and tried to think logically. She didn't even know why he was coming or what he wanted. He kept veering between wanting to be friends and then talking to her in a very explicit sexual way. It left her feeling confused and irritated. Orla got in the bath with the taps still running and scrubbed herself violently. She disappeared under the water, feeling surreal. Sometimes she felt like her life was happening to someone else. Sometimes she held her breath under the water and wondered what it would feel like to just stay there. Drift away. Not have to think any more. She had read somewhere that drowning was the most painful way to die. Orla jerked herself upright to stop this dangerous train of thought and applied herself to the task in hand. She buffed herself dry with the rather beautiful Indian cotton towels she had treated herself to last month, slathered on body butter and lay on the bed, breathless, waiting for it to absorb.

The Blackberry flashed red again.

"I'm in Cambridge. I'm lost. I need directions."

"Cambridge! You've gone too far. You need the A14."

Orla proceeded to direct him awkwardly to her tiny village in the midst of East Anglia. She didn't have a good sense of direction and was worried he would think she was an idiot. Orla was not a clever, logical corporate lawyer like his wife. She worked out she had about half an hour in which to finish getting dressed. She opened the bottom drawer of her dressing table and pulled out a box. Inside, still wrapped in the tissue paper, was some black lingerie she had bought six months ago and never wore. It was a black lace and satin chemise: all in one with matching black stockings. Orla regarded it nervously, fingering the material, feeling afraid to actually wear it. She screwed up her courage and put it on, followed by the stockings. She laughed to herself when she realised she had no full-length mirror to admire herself in, only a small makeup mirror. Orla looked down at the lace flowers and thought how beautiful the chemise was, how special it made her feel. She wasn't so pleased with the bump of her stomach, which protruded out instead of being flat like those of models in magazines. Orla hoped Nathaniel wouldn't mind. She didn't really know what he liked. She smoothed her hands over the chemise, over the curves of her body, and told herself that she was beautiful. She enjoyed the exquisite smoothness of the satin and the bumps of the lace flowers. She roused herself from the dream she was slipping into and threw on the sweater dress; then she zipped up her black leather boots. Her makeup case was looking forlorn and neglected. There was hardly anything in it. Orla went into the bathroom and tried to make up her face as best she could with the remnants of her old cosmetics, peering into the tiny mirror to see if she had smudged her lipstick. She wasn't quite sure if she looked good or not. The girlish arts had never really been a strong point with Orla. She sprayed herself with too much perfume and attempted to straighten her wavy hair with the metal straighteners she hadn't had out since Christmas.

She heard a loud rap on the front door, which was repeated three times. There was no doorbell.

There he was, standing in the doorway. Orla took an intake of breath at how attractive she found him and felt a contraction deep inside herself. Her body was telling her she wanted him. She did want him. He did not look that much different from when she had known him in Edinburgh, possibly his hair was shorter, thinner, and neater, and he was slightly heavier, but really he was much the same. He was as beautiful as ever. It was strange to think of all those years that had passed. So much had changed, and yet nothing had changed. He was too tall to fit into the door without stooping. He gave her a broad smile, which she returned. Images of the past flashed into Orla's mind. Nathaniel had used to come round to the flat to see Oriel, to buy grass and talk about music. He was always with lots of other students: the in-crowd, with too much money to spend, loud voices, and big ideas. They had always been everywhere and done everything—travelling in India, voluntary work in Africa, treks in the Himalayas, rock concerts in New York. Orla was envious of them in a way, but also wary. She was shy and unworldly; Orla had hardly been out of the country; Scotland was the only world she knew, but she longed for other experiences. They were all from the south of England, a place which Orla had never been to at that time. They had a confidence imbued in them from the start, which Scots had never been given. In turns, they fascinated and repulsed her.

Nathaniel had been quiet with her then, and they had never really had a proper conversation. Orla would sit curled on the sofa in Oriel's flat—almost invisible, like a pet cat—while the others talked about bands she had never heard of. She would watch Nathaniel out of the corner of her eye, drinking in his physical perfection while also being irritated with him, the way he was so full of himself, his name-dropping, his pretension. He spent his summer holidays in New York, where he worked in trendy bars and roadied for up-and-coming bands. He had dinner parties in his New Town flat, which his rich parents had bought for him, where exotic things like avocados were served and expensive champagne was drunk. Orla had heard all about them from friends of friends. Orla and Oriel had never been invited to one of these events. At this point in her life, Orla had never been to a dinner party at all, and she had never eaten an avocado. She had seen them in the supermarket but dismissed them as too expensive. Nathaniel was like something from another world. He seemed to take up all the space in whichever room he was in. Orla never thought he would look twice at her. In fact, she knew he had a girlfriend—a tall, willowy blonde with long leather boots who strode about the campus self-confidently. She always made Orla think of a Nazi storm trooper who would come and steal Orla up and place her in a cattle truck for not being perfect enough. Orla had presumed she was not Nathaniel's type. She had presumed wrongly, as it happened.

The bang of the door behind Nathaniel brought Orla to the present, out of the reveries of the past. He held her with such force that she fell to the ground with him on top of her. Orla giggled with the shock of it. She was intensely surprised by how strong his passion seemed; he was literally shaking with it. He had never seemed like this when they had talked on the Internet. Then he was much cooler, almost disinterested. Now he was trembling as he hugged her. Then Nathaniel was kissing her on the mouth, passionately but quite gently. His tongue probed the inside of her mouth, exploring it. Orla felt as if she was drowning in a sensation she had not felt for a long time. She wrapped her legs around him and felt his bare skin underneath his top. His mouth became more insistent, and then he suddenly reared up, made a noise almost like an animal, somewhere between a grunt and a roar, and ripped at her panties until they tore open. Nathaniel was inside her immediately. Orla felt a stab of pain with the shock of it, and then it eased as he went in deeper, changing the angle as he raised himself up. He plunged into her with the force of a wild thing. For once, Orla's mind was swept clean, erased as she gave herself to the physical. The moment seemed to be lasting eternally until he finally collapsed on top of her, laying his head on her breasts, sweating. Orla lay gasping, still shocked, a handful of his light hair in her fist.

After a few minutes, he raised his head and smiled at her. "Sorry, it was too rough. I just wanted you so much."

"No, it was lovely," Orla answered as she leaned forward to kiss his cheek.

This seemed to please him, as his smile widened. He gathered her up as if she were a small child and carried her through to the bedroom door, went through and rested her on the bed. Nathaniel unzipped Orla's boots and pulled off her tights and what remained of her panties. He lifted the dress over her head and unhooked her bra. He kissed her again. Then he leaned back and looked at her for a full minute. Orla smiled up at him slightly nervously. She felt almost afraid of him and unsure what he expected. She found him insanely attractive and was still amazed he was in her bed. Nathaniel leaned forward and kissed her firmly on the mouth. She could taste something, not unpleasant, on his breath that she couldn't place.

Orla wrapped her legs right around him, and they bucked on the bed like young horses on the first spring grass. Then he was suddenly inside her again, deeper and deeper. She felt waves of pleasure spread through her as sounds came from her mouth. Without warning, he suddenly withdrew and flipped her over. She felt his cock probing her anus, exploring, finding a way in. Then he found the doorway and was inside her ass. Orla felt a sensation of pleasure and pain like she had never felt before. Somewhere, her mind registered the shock that she was having anal sex, which was a first for her. She could hear Nathaniel roaring like some wild beast as he finally came inside her. He rolled off and lay sweating and breathless beside Orla. She lay quietly for some minutes and then propped herself up on his chest. She fingered his skin, which was still hot and wet. Nathaniel smiled widely at her and stated, "That was very naughty." He kissed her briefly on the mouth and asked for a shower. Orla explained she didn't have one and heaved herself up to pour him the bath.

He followed her into the bathroom and laughed at the sight of the gargantuan tub. Orla turned the taps on full and apologised for it. "It takes ages to fill." Orla felt slightly embarrassed at what to do, so she left him to it and got dressed in the bedroom. Then she returned to the kitchen and made some more coffee, finding comfort in the rich smell as it brewed. She sat in the armchair and waited for him, feeling dazed but surprised at the feeling of contentment that had overtaken her. After what seemed like an eternity, Nathaniel appeared in front of her, dressed and smiling. Her heart seemed to jump at the sight of him—literally leaping like in the saying. These were all new sensations for Orla. She jumped up and hugged him without thinking. They embraced for many moments, and he kissed the back of her neck.

"I've got to go. Sorry. It's a family thing. Boring but I have to be there."

"OK," Orla squeaked, trying not to show her disappointment. She had hoped he would stay and talk to her for a little longer.

So he went.

CHAPTER EIGHT

Orla spent the rest of the day as if in a dream. She was amazed by how elevated her mood had become simply by the act of having sex with Nathaniel. Joy seemed to radiate through her entire being. She felt like sunshine was literally pouring out of her. Orla had not felt like this for *years*. Her little seed of hope seemed to have germinated, sprouted, and spread like a wild vine throughout her whole body. She felt whole, complete, full of hope for the future. It was as if an old door in a Victorian kitchen garden wall, long rusted shut and covered with ivy, had been broken open by the new garden boy, revealing a rich, luxuriant, overgrown patch of greenery—verdant, bursting with fruit and flowers and life. Orla was standing at the edge of the door, peeking in, hopeful of more treasures within.

With the joyful feeling came an excess of energy. She cleaned the house with unusual zeal, buffing the kitchen taps until they shone and rearranging the spice cupboard with military precision. Usually, she was slovenly about such things. She needed to have a bath, but she was reluctant. She wanted the smell of him to stay on her for as long as possible. It made her feel as if a part of him was still with her. She found, to her ridiculous amusement, that she was humming an old Carpenters tune she hadn't heard since childhood. She remembered it on the radio as she played with her dolls on the rug. The gooey lyrics came back to her:

Why do stars suddenly appear
every time you are near?
Just like me, they long to be
close to you.

Normally she would hate this kind of thing, but today it all seemed appropriate. It was like she finally understood what slushy love songs were all about.

Orla pulled on her coat and went walking. She strode up the lane and turned to walk along the side of the beet field, which was brown stubble at this time of year. The landscape was still stark with winter, but nothing could dampen Orla's mood today. The sky was white, a blank, crowning the dark, drained earth. The trees reached upwards, as if naked and forgotten by the sun. She stopped to feel the bark of an oak tree, enjoying the roughness underneath her fingers and then hugging it, putting her cheek close as if trying to listen for a heartbeat. "I love Nathaniel," she told the tree with a conspiratorial air. Orla almost skipped along, climbing the fence into the next field and sending the rabbits asunder before her. She turned her face up to the grey, huge East Anglian sky. Usually, she did not like the flat openness of the country and the vastness above her, but today she saw it almost as if for the first time. She felt its freedom. She used to feel uncomfortable by the fact that you could see too far, but today she didn't mind seeing too far. She wanted to see too far: right over the rainbow. She wanted to see the bluebirds. Orla laughed at herself and the *Wizard of Oz* imagery in her head. She realised that she had been sad for a very long time, and a simple act of love had made her happy. An act of love or perhaps an act of sex? A sliver of ice planted itself in her chest and made her shudder. No! She would not think like that. She loved Nathaniel and Nathaniel loved her. Orla was thinking positively like all the self-help gurus said. She refused to listen to her shadow, which was trying to whisper that they had hardly spoken to each other, that it had all been about sex…Orla shook her head. *No.* Today she was not going to listen to these thoughts. She turned abruptly and almost ran home. At the doorway, she noticed some tiny daffodils were starting to bud, a smudge of yellow in the brown of the winter garden. She hugged herself with delight.

Spring was coming, and hope.

CHAPTER NINE

Orla passed through the following week in a dream—but a dream that made her feel good. She was full of life and sparkle. Orla laughed uproariously at jokes that weren't that funny and sang tunes to herself as she marked the interminable books. She taught her lessons on autopilot but with a renewed enthusiasm and rushed home to dream about Nathaniel. She gave Elijah short shrift—ignored him. He followed her around with puppy-dog eyes and a defeated air. She hardened her heart and kept him at arm's length. It was unhealthy to be so close to him, she told herself; she felt relieved she had found a diversion. Each evening, she checked Facebook for a message from Nathaniel.

None came.

She made excuses for him. He was busy. He was away on a business trip. His wife was snooping on him. He was playing it cool so as not to seem too keen. He came to her each night in her dreams, his face hovering above her, kissing her deliciously on the face and neck. She felt total peace during these dreams, as if wrapped in a thick, soft blanket. These dreams kept her in hope.

On Friday evening, she cracked. She had poured herself a large glass of Spanish Rioja, had a luxurious bath, and lathered herself with chocolate-flavoured body butter. She perched next to the Aga with the laptop on her knee. Orla logged on to Facebook and looked at Nathaniel's page. He had added a few more friends but had not written anything. He had been on but had not messaged her. She felt irritated. He wasn't that busy—just too busy for Orla. She felt the familiar cold chill of despair rise up from the pit of her stomach, through her body, and down her arms. It was a physical ache.

An ache she had felt before many times.

Orla took a sip of the wine and closed her eyes. She felt her tears sliding down her face. She had failed. He didn't like her. She wondered what it was. The sex? Maybe she was a bad lay or whatever people said. Orla didn't know. She had tried her best. She had let him do everything he wanted. It didn't appear to be good enough. The frigid comment made by her first boyfriend still haunted her. She took things to heart. Orla never forgot anything. All her wrongs she wrapped round herself like cords that she couldn't free herself from. They held her down and prevented her from being what she really could be. She wondered if it was something else. He didn't like her as a person? That was worse. She supposed she wasn't interesting enough. He had thought her life too simple, too provincial. She was a boring schoolteacher, after all. Orla didn't have a flashy life or go to parties or drink champagne. She didn't know the right people. All her life she had felt herself on the outside looking in, looking at other people having good lives. Somehow she didn't know how to join in. She had tried hard all week not to message him, but it hadn't worked. Orla didn't know what to do.

She wrote, "I really enjoyed seeing you last week. Your body was amazing. I miss you. I love you. xxx."

Orla regarded the message critically. Maybe it was all wrong. She didn't know. She sent it anyway. What else could she do? She sat staring at the screen. Her head felt full of cotton wool. She couldn't think straight. It had felt so right with Nathaniel. She had felt sure he had liked her. He had been so passionate. Now it felt all wrong. After ten minutes, she accepted the fact that he wasn't online and wasn't going to reply. She slammed shut the lid and placed the laptop on the floor. Orla opened the door of the Aga to watch the flames dance. In the yellow and orange, she saw figures playing and laughing and dancing. Other people. Happy people. Laughing at her. She wished she could be inside the fire with them. Wished that she could be anywhere but here. Orla wondered why she was being punished. What had she done wrong? Did God hate her? She had tried to be good, but inside she felt there was something bad. Something that made her do stupid things—things like marrying the most unsuitable man in Edinburgh and like having an inappropriate friendship with a teenage boy.

Orla carried on in this pointless vein for two weeks. Every evening, she checked her Facebook for a message from Nathaniel. Every evening there was none. She went through her days robotically, barely seeing, barely hearing, paying no attention. She avoided Elijah. She cancelled his lessons, saying he had caught up. She stopped jogging with him, saying she had joined a gym, which was a lie. She lunched with the younger children. Her loneliness entrapped her like steel bands. It was all her fault, she said to herself. She had brought it on herself. She was punished. Eventually, she unfriended Nathaniel on Facebook.

It was finished.

She felt he had used her. She was another notch in the bedpost. She had fallen for it completely. Orla damned her naivety. It was something that she had never understood about men. They could be intimate with you and then drop you like a stone. It had happened to her at university before Oriel. Men just wanted the conquest with nothing emotional. She hadn't understood it then, and she didn't now. Sex had nothing to do with love. It was just sex.

Like animals. Maybe that's all we were. Maybe she had got it all wrong, thinking that there could be finer things, finer emotions. Orla had tried to be normal. She had tried to have a relationship. She had failed. She wouldn't even have minded if it had been an affair. It would have been better than the vast, featureless nothing that she felt certain lay ahead of her.

The unravelling, already begun, proceeded further.

CHAPTER TEN

In the past, during times of despair, Orla had thrown herself into her work. She couldn't seem to do this anymore. Her anger at the school, the staff, and the management grew and grew like a hard lump inside her. She had been used in love, and now she felt used at work. Men half her age, straight out of college, had been promoted ahead of her. Others were praised at the staff meetings. Orla was ignored. She had done so much for the school over the years—reorganising things, trying to make order from chaos, trying to raise the pitiful academic standards, trying to improve the severe lack of motivation in the boys—but her efforts were not appreciated. The new head of prep seemed determined to bully her. He belittled her at every opportunity. Orla didn't know why. She didn't understand it. She was just trying her best. Maybe at some level he was afraid of her. Blenkinsopp was a little man with a little mind. He bullied his pretty but obtuse and timid stay-at-home wife. Even the staff commented on it. One evening, Orla had attended a dull drinks party in his back garden when his wife confided she did not know what to do with a garden, as she had never had one.

Before he had become head, they had lived in a flat in the upper school boarding house.

Blenkinsopp had overheard this remark and roared at her, "Then you best learn, woman." The assembled teachers were stunned into silence.

The boys loved Orla, it was true, but their opinion counted for nothing. Presumably, Blenkinsopp was of the view that all women should stay at home, have babies, and mind their manners. Orla had a sharp mind, was outspoken, and had strong views on education. Blenkinsopp did not share them. To him, a good school was signified by polished shoes, short hair, and success on the rugby field. Nothing else seemed important to him. He was edging Orla out.

A series of events confirmed Orla in this view. She had a complaint from a parent that the homework she set was too hard. As usual, she was not supported. The parent didn't even come to see her but talked to the head of department. A letter of apology was written without consulting her. She had an argument with the same head of department about the use of the comma. The man had a degree in law, not in English. He was a pedant with no creativity. Her mark book mysteriously disappeared from her desk the day before it was due to be handed in for checking. The boys reported that Heathcote-Jones had openly mocked her Scottish accent in one of his music lessons. Eventually, she was hauled in to Blenkinsopp's office for a two-hour meeting about her attitude and evident unhappiness. Her class were left unsupervised and ran riot on the first floor.

Orla sat in the office and looked at the oak panelling, the bucolic art, the antique lampshades. It was like the Queen Mother's boudoir, she thought. This was where all the money was spent, obviously. Not on books for the English Department. Priorities were strange. The only thing that mattered was how things looked on the surface. It wasn't a philosophy Orla could subscribe to anymore. It was the room of a small man trying to be something he wasn't, showing off to the parents, trying to pretend he was one of them. The room was completely devoid of personal taste. It was just an imitation of what people thought upper-class homes looked like. A part of Orla realised this suggested he had underneath his bluster a complete lack of confidence in himself. The thought also struck her that he had never once mentioned which university he had been to or even what he had studied.

Orla sat in the overstuffed chair and regarded him levelly. He was actually one of the few older members of staff who was not overweight. This was due to the fact that he went running every morning, and his wife was a health freak who probably cooked him low-calorie meals. They were physically fit and appeared to have an outdoorsy, almost military regime. Strength through joy was how Orla thought of it. His dress was as conventional as possible: highly polished brown brogues and sports jacket. He was obsessed with sport, and that was all he seemed interested in for the school. Academic attainment seemed to be low in the priority list. She had already had pointless arguments with him about the low literacy skills and what to do about it. He wasn't interested. The new head of English, promoted above Orla, had done nothing about any of it. His predecessor, a lazy old dragon who had gone off to another school, had done nothing about it. Nobody cared. What really annoyed Orla was that in spite of all the money and energy devoted to sporting prowess, Northwold always languished at the bottom of the local league. They rarely won anything and mostly would be thrashed by the other public schools. Orla noticed Blenkinsopp's hair was heavily greying, and she noted again with irritation the ridiculous little quiff he had at the front, which always made her think of a warped version of Tintin. The strain of headship was showing on him already. He had visibly shrivelled in the last year, and she realised from his croaky voice that he had a bad cold. She did not feel any pity for him. There had been too many instances where he had put her down just for the sake of it and made comments about her clothes and shoes. He was a bully.

He began, "Well, Orla, we don't seem to be very happy, do we?" Orla thought, *Who is this "we"?*

She decided to tell him. "I am unhappy about many things. I am unhappy at the way the English Department is being run. There are no new schemes of work, there are not enough books or other resources, and there is no strategy. Nothing has been done. Are you aware that a quarter of the upper third have a reading age below eight even though they are about to take Common Entrance? Discipline is sliding. The system does not appear to work. How can it be said to work when Fraser has had ten detentions this term and his behaviour is no different? I believe it states somewhere in the policy document that after three detentions a boy is to be suspended. As far as I am aware, this has not happened."

She looked him in the eye and waited.

"Orla, I can't do anything about the head of department position now."

"I am not complaining that I was not made head of department. I just want things to work. Currently, they don't," said Orla.

Blenkinsopp sighed and began a sermon. "Orla, it seems our little school is too small for ambitions such as yours. Perhaps you should seek a deputy head position elsewhere. I would be happy to recommend you. I do, of course, know all the heads in the area and many further afield. My advice is that you should stop caring."

He droned on in this vein for what seemed to be an eternity. Orla couldn't get much of a word in edgewise. When she tried, she was told off for interrupting. She stopped listening. All her head was doing was repeating the phrase *stop caring* over and over again. What sort of an attitude was that? She hadn't come into teaching to stop caring. Orla began to wish she had gone to work in a bank. Eventually, when there appeared to be a lull in the monologue, she thanked him and left. It was all pointless. She was being edged out.

Stop caring.

Then something happened that meant she could stand it no longer.

She was sitting in the lunch hall late on a Wednesday afternoon, avoiding everyone. Most of the children were at matches, so there was hardly anybody there. Surprisingly, Elijah walked in and went to the counter. As ever, she had sensed he was there before she saw him. It was unusual that he wasn't at a match. Orla turned her gaze away from him determinedly and concentrated on chewing her food. Within moments, he was sitting opposite her, looking nervous and awkward.

"What's the matter?" he asked eventually, his eyes drilling into her in that way she found so disconcerting.

"Nothing, I am perfectly fine," she replied, looking at him fiercely.

"I thought you…liked me," he returned, pausing at the word *like* as if it wasn't quite right.

"Of course I like you. I like all the children."

"You've been avoiding me. I thought…I thought…you loved me."

He kept staring straight into her eyes. Orla could not admit the truth. She had gone into fight mode. She was angry at the whole world, including Elijah. Angry at him for making her love him when she had tried so hard not to. Angry at him for resurrecting her deeply buried feelings. Angry at him for penetrating her carefully constructed fences.

"Elijah. I don't love you, and I never will," she shot back at him with venom, her eyes flashing with anger.

His mouth trembled and his eyes filled with tears. He looked down at the table for some minutes and appeared fascinated by a little pile of salt, which he kept fingering with intense concentration. Orla thought he was going to cry, but he recovered himself and looked levelly at her again.

"OK," he managed. "I wanted to tell you something anyway. Something quite difficult."

She kept staring back at him, becoming frightened of what might be coming.

"It's Rupert. He told me something…about Heathcote-Jones. He said sometimes in the boarding house, he asks Rupert to come to his room, and then once he went and had sweets and stuff… but then he asked him to do things…you know, like rude things. I wanted to tell you."

Orla felt irritation rise so highly in her that she thought her head might just blow off. She covered her face with her hands. Of course, she had always suspected it. It had never come out in the open as clearly as this before. Rupert. Poor, unspeaking, depressed, friendless Rupert. She had failed to protect him. She should have known. She should have listened to the instinct that told her what Heathcote-Jones was like. Orla had pushed the thought away, ignored it. She felt cold guilt mix with her hot anger.

Orla got up from the table without speaking. She went to her room and fired an email off to Neil Blenkinsopp detailing the conversation she had just had. He replied after about half an hour, saying he would look into it.

It took him more than a week to look into it. The reply, when it came, was late on a Friday evening. Orla was at her desk, marking as usual. As she read it, Orla felt her blood turn ice cold, as if something evil had got inside her.

Dear Miss McKenzie,

I have interviewed Rupert about your concerns and also Mr Heathcote-Jones. Rupert agrees that nothing inappropriate has occurred and that he was asked to do extra practise for the forthcoming singing concert by Mr Heathcote-Jones. Rupert is stressed about the Exams in which his father has expressed a wish for him to do well, and that is why he has seemed unhappy.

Orla sent him her resignation with immediate effect by email. She shut down the computer, picked up her coat and handbag, turned out the light, and walked downstairs and then outside into the blackness of the car park. She could barely see to put her key in the lock of her Mini. She got in and started the engine. Then she sat for a few minutes in total silence. Orla felt nothing. Emptiness. She knew there was nothing she could do. The management were too powerful for her to stand against. She would not be able to protect Rupert. The men were standing together, covering up for each other. She steered the car out of the car park and round to the exit road. She passed the ugly brick boarding house building, and she could see some of the boys playing an impromptu game of rugby. As her headlights picked them out, she realised she would never see them again.

On the way home, Orla stopped off at the off-licence in town and bought a bottle of Laphroaig malt whisky. At home, she opened the top and gulped a mouthful straight out of the bottle. She enjoyed the burn as it went down her throat and the taste of peat and smoke. The taste of home—a long way from here. She sat down on the floor in the kitchen, cradling the bottle between her legs and glugging some of the precious liquid every few minutes. She wanted oblivion, not to feel. She had lost her job, she had lost Nathaniel, she had lost Elijah. She felt that she had hit the bottom. Orla closed her eyes and continued drinking. Eventually, with most of the bottle gone, her eyes went out of focus and she could not think of anything anymore. That was what she had wanted. She collapsed onto the floor, her head against the wooden boards. She revived herself for a moment, grabbed the overturned bottle, and poured the remains of it over her head. It dripped down her hair and onto her face, a replacement for the tears that would not come. She heard herself scream: a strange, unearthly noise. The blackness finally came as she hit unconsciousness.

Orla welcomed the zero.

CHAPTER ELEVEN

Orla spent the following week in bed. Well, that was not strictly true. She got up to stoke the Aga, to turn the heater to maximum, to urinate, to drink water. The rest of the time, she curled in the bed in a cocoon. She ignored the insistent beep of her phone until it turned itself off. She ignored the slap of the letters falling through the letter box. Most of the time, she slept. She dreamed a recurring dream. She was flailing around in a sea of mud. A plank of wood was thrust towards her. She couldn't see who was thrusting it. Orla tried to grab it, but she kept missing. Then the plank was removed, and she felt herself sink into the mud. When she woke in between dreams, she felt that her head was encased in a metal helmet that was pressing on her brain, and all she heard was a black thud. Sometimes she retched into the sink but nothing came—nothing but bile. Sometimes she dreamed of Nathaniel, of the weight of his body pressing into her. Sometimes she dreamed of Elijah, his disembodied face always smiling up at her. Occasionally, the faces of the staff of Northwold would make an appearance—contorted into evil expressions with sneering smiles. Hatred would rise within her and make her buck in the bed with the force of it. Orla would hear voices calling her name: sometimes quiet, sometimes loud, sometimes kind, sometimes mocking. She didn't know if they were really there or illusion. Orla wondered if she would die in the bed. She asked God to kill her. She prayed for it. She couldn't see any reason to go on. She had nobody to care for, and nobody cared for her. Given this, she didn't see a point in being alive. She had failed as a person, failed in her career, failed in her relationships, failed to protect Rupert, failed to improve Elijah's attainment, failed to capture Nathaniel's heart. She couldn't do anything right. She didn't think she would ever be able to leave the bed.

On the seventh day, she woke one morning just before the dawn. She felt different. Her head wasn't banging. For the first time, she felt hungry. Her cat, Grimalkin, was pawing at her face.

Oh my God, she thought. She hadn't fed him. She felt his ribs. He felt fat enough. Of course he was not stupid. He would have hunted or, more likely, scavenged from the neighbours. He was resourceful, independent.

Orla rushed to the kitchen, poured the dry cat food into a bowl, and then filled up Grimalkin's water. He attacked the meal with vigour. She felt guilty. One creature had needed her at least. Orla made herself coffee and felt it reviving her as it slipped down her throat and warmed her insides. She looked down at her still naked body and saw that she had lost weight. Her stomach was finally flat: a long-held ambition. She laughed at the ridiculousness of the thought. She laughed at her own ridiculousness. The reedy light of the dawn made her look to the window. Orla went out into the garden, still completely naked. She knelt down and rubbed her face in the wet grass. She laughed again, enjoying the feeling that she was a mad old hag, something out of Macbeth. Orla lay down on her back and spread her legs and arms out wide as she smiled up at the sky. She wasn't upset anymore. She was free. She was free of that horrible school, free of all that exhausting work, free of all those nasty, judgemental, jealous people. She could do whatever she wanted. She would never teach again, she told herself. The thought held a certain delight. No more downtrodden, sensible schoolteacher. Orla would be an insane witch lady, a woman of the woods. She could live by foraging, poaching, and stealing. Anything was possible. She laughed again at the madness of her thoughts, but they also delighted her. Even though the delight surged in her, there was the gnawing guilt that she had left Rupert behind, abandoned him to goodness knew what fate. She didn't know what to do. Rashly, she rang up the NSPCC helpline and left an anonymous message about Northwold, Rupert, and Heathcote-Jones. She didn't expect anything to come of it, but there was a slight easing of her guilt.

Life could begin.

CHAPTER TWELVE

The following day, Orla dressed herself in a blue skirt-suit, applied a thin layer of makeup, and drove into town to the job centre. She didn't eat any breakfast, as there was nothing left in the house that hadn't gone rotten. She hadn't ever been in one of these places before. It was anodyne, with purple seating and cream walls. She wandered around nervously, not quite knowing what to do. Then she noticed people were standing in front of little screens, looking at descriptions of the jobs. She felt sorry for the people. They had a resigned, defeated air about them. One man in particular caught her eye. He was maybe sixty, with long, lank, grey hair parted in the centre and an old grey suit that had seen better days. His shirt was grimy around the collar. Orla speculated that he was an alcoholic. She couldn't imagine anyone would want to employ him, poor soul. Orla found a vacant screen and figured out how to use it. Most of the vacancies sounded horrendous. You could flip burgers, clean offices, cold call people to sell things they wouldn't want. Even the worst-sounding positions wanted experience. Orla had never done anything other than teach. She had no experience. Nobody would want her. Then she saw one: groom. This was something that Orla could do. She had been a horsey child and had once worked in a hunting yard on Exmoor in the summer holidays, before hunting had been made illegal. It seemed like fate that it was there.

Orla went to the desk to ask about it. She talked to the adviser about the job. He read out the information listlessly, adding nothing else. He had bad acne and dark, greasy hair. He didn't look much older than Elijah, she thought. "*Stop* thinking about Elijah," she shouted at herself internally.

The boy-man rang up the owner of the stable and talked to someone for a while. Orla was given an appointment for later that very day. How easy it all was. Escape from Northwold.

Orla was now ravenous but buoyed with the success of her first venture into the world after Northwold. She had lunch in one of the big coffee chains in town. She didn't really like it—it seemed too American in feel. There were big fake leather sofas to sit on. The cup of coffee Orla ordered was enormous but tasted cheap and bitter. She poured in several packets of sugar to make it palatable. She had also ordered a ham and cheese panini and a huge chocolate brownie. She enjoyed the food—after her long fast, everything tasted better. The chocolate was a particular treat that she had used to deny herself. Orla found the sweetness intoxicating. She leaned back on the fake leather sofa she had chosen and surveyed the other customers. There were women with small children and single men hunched over laptops. The women were talking with those voices that sounded like they were from London. A Suffolk accent was rarely heard in town these days. Everyone seemed to have migrated here from somewhere else. Orla felt like she had got out of gaol. She had got free. She was a normal person. She was one of these people who had coffee in the middle of the day in town. She was *not* a teacher. Orla laughed out loud with delight. A few people looked over at her in surprise. She didn't care.

Orla drove to the stables. To her surprise, it was an upmarket stud farm, breeding thoroughbreds for racing. Orla drove through the grand entrance gates feeling some trepidation. She had had enough of smart people. She just wanted something ordinary. The place was immaculate. There were little paddocks fenced in with expensive post-and-rail fencing. She could see beautiful, elegant horses out in rugs for daily exercise, their flanks shining in the sun. To her relief, when she met the stable manager, she discovered he was not smart at all. He was Irish, with a beautiful, gentle lilt to his voice, unkempt grey hair, and thin legs. When he shook her hand, she could see black dirt ingrained in his fingernails. He was wearing jeans and big old leather boots topped off with a home-knitted blue Arran jumper that was too big for him. Orla liked him instantly. He was called Sean.

She followed him into the office, which was very neat and orderly, though tiny. Orla sat opposite him on a wooden stiff-backed chair and felt nervous. She had always been rubbish at interviews, her old girlhood shyness returning and making the words tumble out haphazardly until she ended up saying things that she didn't mean at all. She could tell he thought it was odd that she wanted to be a groom and not a teacher.

He began, "So, Orla, tell me about yourself."

She felt terrified but forced herself to speak. "Well...here is my CV." She thrust the piece of half-crumpled paper across to him. "As you can see, I have always been a teacher...but...well...I need a change. I want to downshift, have something less stressful..."

Sean regarded her resume with increasingly widening eyes. Orla knew her qualifications were too impressive for this job. He wouldn't want her.

He looked across at her and asked, "Do you have any experience with horses?"

"Oh yes, when I was a child I was always riding, and I helped out at the local riding school in the holidays. And in my gap year between school and university, I worked at a hunting yard on Exmoor. I am sure I could do it," she gabbled.

Sean leaned back in the chair and searched her eyes.

"You realise the pay won't be very much. It's minimum wage, I am afraid."

"No. That's fine. I don't expect anything else. I just want to work."

He smiled. She smiled.

She got the job. Could it really be this easy?

Orla realised Sean was as bad at interviewing as she was at being interviewed.

So Orla's new life began. The job was only part time. She went in the mornings and mucked out the mares, groomed them, let them out and in from the paddocks, adjusted their rugs, and fed them. They were waiting for their foals to come. The afternoons, she could go home. The pay was really low, but Orla didn't mind. She had enough to cover her rent and a tiny bit left over for food and wine. It was enough. Nobody asked her anything. They were animal people, not people people. Orla liked it. The work was physical and hard, but the change was welcome. She inhaled the sweet smell of the hay as she squashed it into the nets, and she nuzzled her face against the mares' necks, feeling their velvet against her. As the weeks passed, she felt muscles harden in her arms and legs. The work invigorated her. She didn't have to think. She felt better than she had for years. Orla spent her afternoons reading and pottering around the house and garden. She planned a vegetable plot, thinking that if she could grow her own food, it would be cheaper. She was managing. She told herself she was fine. She didn't look at Facebook, she burned letters that appeared stamped from Northwold School. She turned off her phone. Orla wanted to be alone. It was better. Safer.

Orla was fine.

CHAPTER THIRTEEN

Weeks passed. It was almost Easter. Spring was in full swing, and Orla had managed to convince herself that she was having a normal life. The stress of her old life fell away from her; she was like a grass snake shedding its skin. Occasionally, in bed at night, feelings of regret would swallow her, and she would cry into the pillow. She still dreamed of Elijah and of Nathaniel, but the easy routine of her new life comforted her. It was wonderful to be away from the small-mindedness of those people, their shallowness, their materialism. From a distance, she could see the school for the farce it had been. She didn't need to worry anymore. She wasn't a part of it. It was not her problem. She didn't have to care. It was all somebody else's problem.

But Orla was still lonely.

She told herself that this was how it was supposed to be. This was her destiny. Some people got married and had children, and some people didn't. That was how it was. Perhaps there was a purpose for Orla. She didn't know what it was, but maybe it would come to her. She started praying again, started reading the Bible and trying to be good. She rediscovered old poetry: Manley Hopkins, Dickinson, Thomas, Hughes, Rosetti. Orla now had time to read, time to herself. She went for long walks in the flat fields and made herself economical meals from seasonal vegetables and stolen game that Frank gave her. Life gained a comforting rhythm. There was Orla. There was weather and land. There was food and there was wine. There were the mares. Sometimes she sat in the old village church, comforted by being there. Orla wanted God to speak to her, but he seemed far away. Funny how she had felt so close to him as a child. Now she wasn't. She wondered if it was because of all the bad things she had done. She waited. Things would get better.

Everything was fine.

One Sunday afternoon was unseasonably mild. There was a hot spell. Orla had splurged out on a padded garden chair to take advantage of the weather. She donned a pair of denim cut-off shorts, set the chair to maximum recline, and soaked up the sun. Orla had finally begun to relax, to take succour from life, to enjoy small, sensuous pleasures. She began reading a trashy thriller to fit in with her carefree mood. Occasionally, she took a sip of Rioja and worked her way through a bowl of cherries she had bought yesterday in town. Life was good. Orla felt deliciously happy. She had become used to her own company.

The thought struck her to get her laptop. She had not looked at it for weeks. She had had an idea to start writing a journal. She flipped open the lid and for some reason decided to open Facebook. She had given it up since Nathaniel. She clicked open her page, and to her surprise she had fifty-two messages. Intrigued, she looked more closely and realized that they were all from children at school. Friend requests, plaintive missives saying how much they missed her, moans that the new teacher was boring, guilty ramblings about things they had done wrong, endless declarations of love and affection. Orla was stunned by them. She had not expected this. There were even some from parents saying how she had been the best teacher and that they were so sorry she had gone, how much she had inspired their children to love literature. Orla felt tears slip from her eyes. She realised that she had blotted all of this out, tried not to think about it. She had missed the boys terribly but had not let herself think about them. She had created armour to protect herself from this feeling.

There were ten messages from Elijah.

Orla opened them tentatively. The first few asked where she was, why she had left, what she was doing. The next few told her he loved her. They became increasingly frustrated and angry. The final one read: "Why don't you reply? Fuck you you bitch!"

Orla sighed. The feeling of love he had always managed to create in her continued—a pang of longing for communion. She didn't mind the angry words. She understood it. He had a passionate nature, as she did. The depth of feeling was obvious, along with the desperation to connect with her in some way that the others also felt to a much lesser degree. Recklessly, she added them all as friends. She replied to every message, saying she couldn't explain why she had left but that she had wanted to help someone and it had all gone wrong, that she missed them too, that they must be good and do their best. Elijah she left until last:

> I am really sorry. I just tried to help Rupert. They wouldn't listen. They wouldn't do anything. It's not your fault. I miss you of course. Just be good. I am fine. I've got a job with horses. It's fun. Don't be upset. Xxx

Orla thought that would be that.

The messages had perturbed her mood. They were all so sweet, as they had always been. How could they turn into such horrible adults? There had been no contact from any colleagues. None of the adults had cared about her—only the boys. It was a strange fact. She seemed to scare people away, intimidate them, but the children were different. They saw something else. Orla didn't understand it.

And then there was Elijah. She did not regard him as a child. He had always been too self-assured for that. The strength of his feeling was obvious in the messages with their increasing frustration. It was a strange thing…another thing she could not understand. It seemed Orla did not understand anything anymore. She could not teach anyone anything. She had no answers, only questions.

Orla went in and lay down on her bed. She fell into a fitful, uneasy sleep where long arms reached out to her over a great abyss. She felt she flew to a strange place. She was looking down. Boys were walking into a building along a stone ramp. Some odd machine was chopping off parts of them—arms and legs, hands, ears. Blood spurted from the severed areas. They did not cry or flinch. They just kept on walking into the building. Then they would emerge from the other side, and the whole thing would happen again.

A strange dream.

CHAPTER FOURTEEN

Communication with Elijah resumed. She spent her mornings at her job, her afternoons pottering in the house or garden, and her evenings curled up with her laptop, talking to Elijah. The sense of danger she had always felt about their friendship melted away. After all, she wasn't a teacher anymore; it was just writing, and it was harmless, she told herself. In truth, she needed him as much as he appeared to need her. He was her link with humanity, with the outside world she had left behind, the world beyond her own head.

Elijah's conversation was usually light-hearted and jokey. It cheered Orla up immensely. He could lift her spirits so easily. They talked of many things. He moaned about the teachers, bragged about his performance in rugby matches, related tricks the boys had got up to. He never once mentioned his schoolwork. Orla liked this. She wasn't a teacher anymore. She enjoyed not being responsible, not caring. Their online friendship was very much as it had been in real life. They talked easily. It seemed as if each intuitively knew what the other wanted from the interaction. Sunlight entered Orla's mind more permanently. Over time, the conversations became more personal, more intimate. Secrets came out.

One particular Saturday evening, Orla was in her armchair with her legs curled up underneath her. She noticed that the stuffing was coming out of the arm, but it hardly seemed to matter. Nobody would see it anyway. Orla was wearing an old green sweater dress she had bought years ago on holiday in Skye. An elderly American lady with long, unkempt grey hair had knitted it from wool from her own sheep and dyed it with local plants. Orla loved it, as it reminded her of the wild islands she adored. Orla noticed that there was a hole in the sleeve, probably from a moth. She wondered idly how much crofts were to buy. More than Orla could afford, probably. She daydreamed for several minutes about living on Skye in a little croft cottage with her ideal man. Orla had treated herself to a bottle of cheap red wine, which she was slowly sipping while rereading *Wuthering Heights*, probably for the twentieth time. She was in a deliciously naughty mood. Since stopping teaching, it was as if she had discovered some long-hidden parts of herself—her youth, rebelliousness, and sensuality. The person she had been as a student was resurfacing; she was opening like a lotus blossom on a still pond, rediscovering herself. She was her own person now, not what other people wanted her to be. She felt young, like a girl. Elijah helped to make her feel like this. Theirs was no longer a teacher-pupil relationship but simply two people who enjoyed each other's company. He was fifteen. She was thirty-five. But the difference was like nothing when they talked to each other. They were equals. Their very souls seemed to reach out to each other across the distance. Elijah had replaced Nathaniel as the man in Orla's life, the only man there was and the only man she wanted there to be.

Orla closed her novel and reached for her laptop. She flipped it open and logged on to Facebook. Elijah was online, waiting for her, as always. Mostly they talked on the chat facility, but sometimes they messaged each other. Elijah appeared to notice within seconds that she was there.

"Hello baby!"

Orla laughed at the enthusiasm.

"Hi Elijah. How are you?"

"Good, good, good."

He did something to make coloured smiley faces all over the chat box. She didn't know how he did it, and he wouldn't tell her.

"That's very sweet. It makes me smile."

"Nom, nom, nom."

"What?"

"It means I like it. How come you haven't got a boyfriend seeing as you're so beautiful?"

"I'm not beautiful."

"You are."

"Well I was married once, but it didn't work out. I don't really like talking about it."

"Tell me."

"No."

"I wanna know…"

"Well, he was Jamaican. I was very young. We weren't married long. He was no good, really. Then I became a teacher. He wasn't faithful. He gave me VD once."

"Sounds like an asshole."

"Yes, he was."

"I would never do anything like that."

"No, you wouldn't. You are too sweet. You'll meet a girl and get married and it will be lovely."

"I want you though."

"Elijah! Don't say things like that."

"Why not?"

"It's silly."

"No it's not. Do you think I'm good looking?"

"Yes, you are. Very. And you know it."

"Really. No I don't. I'm not muscley enough. Not yet anyway."

"I like that when guys have a six-pack. I think it's hard to get though."

"I've got one of those."

"You have not."

"Have. Wanna see?"

"Well that's not possible. We can't see each other."

"We can."

"No."

"I want to see you. How do you feel when you talk to me?"

"Well, good. Hot. You make me go sweaty…and wet."

"Good."

"OMG I can't believe I said that. Oops. I have had some wine."

"It's fine. Don't stress. You are always drinking."

"I AM NOT!"

"It's OK. I'm teasing. I'm in bed and it's really warm and cosy. I wish you were here with me."

"You are too young, honey."

"No I'm not."

"OK. I've got to go."

Orla closed the lid and thought about the interaction. She should have felt guilty but didn't. It was so easy. It just flowed. She knew it was impossible. It would just have to remain a fantasy. Orla had finally met someone she connected with; yet he was still a child. The world had a cruel irony about it. He made her feel beautiful and sexy and fun and happy and everything all at the same time. He had gained confidence and had started to talk to her more intimately. The old Orla would have stopped it by now. The new Orla was reckless, happy, carefree. She had woken up to her own womanhood, and nothing else seemed to matter. He wasn't exactly the soulmate she had had in mind. He had no interest in books or poetry or anything in that line. He was her opposite. Yet it didn't seem to matter. They got on. Yin and yang.

The shadows had receded...for now.

CHAPTER FIFTEEN

Orla and Elijah continued to talk to each other in this vein over the next few weeks. The weather had mellowed out into a glorious spring. It was very mild, and Orla began to plant things in the garden: carrot seedlings, garlic, lettuces, onions. She felt quite proud of her new bucolic life. She no longer felt the need to buy clothes and shoes. She lived in her jeans and old sweaters. Orla stopped paying attention to the television so she didn't feel the need to enter into the consumer world. Radio 4 was her usual companion, along with old jazz standards from her CD collection.

She was in a cosy cocoon. She was delighted to have lost the stressed, sick feeling that had been her bedfellow for so many years. For Elijah, the Easter holidays were approaching.

Matters progressed one extraordinarily sunny Sunday afternoon. Orla was stretched out on the lounger like a particularly lazy cat, sipping wine and daydreaming about what life might have been like if she hadn't been a teacher. She would have moved to London and got a glamorous job in PR for a champagne house, she decided. She would have dated lots of wealthy, handsome gentlemen and gone to extravagant parties. Rented a little flat in a smart part of town…Notting Hill maybe…small but immaculate: all white. It was a satisfying dream in which she felt successful and beautiful. Orla loosed out her hair from its bun and let it fall around her shoulders. She twisted it between her fingers, enjoying its softness. Orla smiled up at the sun, which was enveloping her in a gentle spring warmth. She was wearing her cut-off jeans shorts and a khaki T-shirt with no bra. She felt the afternoon was perfect. Feeling delicious, she picked her laptop up from the grass and logged on to Facebook. There was a message from Elijah.

"I love you Orla."

He sent her this message every day now. Orla smiled in delight. It made her glow from the inside. She had never felt so cared for, so nurtured. It was a new feeling for Orla. She waited for a few minutes and willed him to come online. To her amazement, he did.

"Hellooooo Orla."

"Hello, Elijah xxx"

"x"

"x"

"What ya doing?"

"Man I AM BORED. Sundays. I'm doing nothing."

"I thought they would have you on a regimented outing."

"Yeah we've done that. Went into town shopping. It was shit."

"It's nearly Easter. Holidays for you. A whole month off. Are you going away?"

"Nah. I'm just going back to the base. Dad's on some trip with a woman he's got. I'm not invited. He's got my mad Aunt Lorelei to look after me. She's deaf and bonkers."

"Hah! Sounds like fun."

"Yeah!"

"So what else?"

"I've been looking at your photos."

"What photos?"

"Holiday ones. I think it's Italy. You are beautiful in them. I've never seen you with your hair down before. It really suits you."

"Oh yes, Italy. I went last summer. To the Amalfi Coast. It was really good. I went on a plane to Naples, stopped over for a few nights, and then got a rickety bus up the coast. I went to Pompeii as well, but it was so hot I mostly just lounged by the hotel pool."

"I like the one of you in the bikini. Your body is beautiful."

"OMG I nearly didn't put that one on. It's a bit racy. The waiter took it."

"I love it. You are so sexy."

"Thanks but you make me feel naughty."

"Good. I want you to be naughty. I've got to go to supper but I want to talk to you tonight. Log on about 10. Promise. x"

"Promise. x"

Orla placed the laptop on the grass and lay back on the lounger. Talking to Elijah always made her feel glowing. He actually thought she was beautiful. Orla couldn't remember anyone saying that to her before. Oriel had never said it. She didn't think Nathaniel had said it either. She smoothed out her hair, playing with its softness. She resolved to buy a colour to cover up the grey streaks. Elijah loved her, and she was beautiful. It was enough. She spent the rest of the afternoon and evening pottering in the garden and kitchen, planting, weeding, making bread. Her heart felt light again, and she hummed while she worked. At nine, she had a luxurious bubble bath and then put on her blue kaftan and returned to the kitchen armchair. She curled herself up waiting for it to be ten. She daydreamed pleasant dreams. Elijah and she lived together in a hot country. They had a white villa with a swimming pool full of clear blue water. They spent their days sunbathing and walking on the beach. Elijah swam in the pool and she watched. They lay together in a double hammock strung between two trees, their limbs entwined around each other, their mouths kissing. It was a wonderful dream. Orla almost started to believe it could come true. Maybe good things could happen to Orla. Maybe.

Ten came, and she logged on to Facebook on the dot. The weather had turned, and Orla could hear the rain dripping on the window and the wind blowing at the fences and trees. She felt cosy and safe in the kitchen, out of the storm. Elijah was already online, waiting for her.

"Helloooo Orla xxx"
"Hello, Elijah. Xxx What are you doing?"
"I'm in bed. I'm supposed to be asleep but I'm under the covers on the phone to you."
"Good. I am glad you are. You always make me smile."
"You make me smile too. :)"
"We make each other happy."
"Yes. I wish you were here in bed with me."
"Oh Elijah, you are too young."
"No I'm not."
"I like being your friend. Don't spoil it."
"Why would I spoil it?"
"People do. I've lost lots of friends."
"I won't spoil it."
"But we can't go too far. Into that area."
"Why not?"
"Because you are a boy."
"I'm not. I'm a man."
"OK. Just love me."

Orla logged off and closed the lid of her laptop. She felt mixed. Part of her was ringing a warning bell in the back of her mind.

It was all getting too intimate. Part of her wanted to go back to the friendship they had had at school…that wonderful, innocent, delightful friendship. Orla knew he wanted more than that. The other, deeper, older, primal part of herself told her that she wanted more too. She was delighted that he loved her, that he wanted her and she wanted him too. Her trust in him had grown. Nobody knew. Nobody would find out. It was just her and Elijah…together forever. He had become her whole world, her lifeline out of the prison of her own mind.

The following week, it was Easter holidays for Elijah. They carried on talking to each other in the afternoons and evenings through Facebook. Every morning, a message of love waited for her.

If he wasn't online, she would send him a message. Otherwise they would talk through the chat facility. There were endless compliments, declarations of love mixed in with chat about everyday, unimportant things. They were very easy with each other. The conversation flowed. They knew just what to say to each other: sometimes serious, sometimes jokey. They never fell out or argued. It seemed perfect. Elijah was charm itself. Orla took a week off work for Easter. She was looking forward to the luxury of doing absolutely nothing. She prayed for sunshine.

Monday dawned clear and bright. A few fluffy clouds were populating the sky, but they didn't look ominous. The sky was azure blue. Optimistically, Orla dragged the lounger into the middle of the lawn and lay down on it wearing denim shorts and a blue polka-dot bikini top.

It was just about warm enough to sunbathe. Orla, being from northerly climes, was quite happy to brave the spring sunshine. She was reading *Lady Chatterley's Lover* by D. H. Lawrence. She had read it before when she was very young but was giving it a revisit. She loved Lawrence—his way of describing things, his accurate view of human behaviour, his frankness about the animal in people. Orla was buried in the book, almost oblivious to everything, when her Blackberry rang. She was surprised, as it very rarely rang these days. She picked it up and was amazed to discover that it was Elijah. She had given him the number some weeks ago in case of emergency, but he had never used it.

"Orla. It's me. Elijah," he said.

"Oh, wow…I'm really shocked. I haven't heard your voice in so long."

He laughed loudly. "Listen. I've had an idea. You're on holiday this week, right? Well, I can give old Aunt Busybody the slip and we can have a staycation together. I can come in the day on my bike, and I'll have to go back in the evening—worse luck. Whaddaya say?"

Orla paused. "Um, what's a staycation?"

"It's where you're on holiday but you stay at home."

"Oh. I don't know about that," Orla said.

"Don't you want to see me?"

"Yes, of course I do. I miss you so much, Elijah."

"Well, there you are then."

"What about your aunt? Won't she wonder where you are?" she asked.

"No. I'll just give her some bullshit about rugby training or something. She won't know. She's always drunk on gin. I'm having a try-out for the county, you know. Rugby. I am awesome."

"Ha! And modest too. OK, OK. I can't believe you are coming."

"Right. Brilliant. We start tomorrow. I'll see you bright and early. Don't sleep in. I love you, babe."

He hung up abruptly. Orla was in shock. He was really coming, really coming to her house. Her doubts disappeared. She felt no trepidation, no worry. It just felt totally natural, wonderful…like it was supposed to be happening. Orla went back to her book in a daze of happiness. She felt no need to frantically clean the house or beautify herself. Elijah would love her just as she was—she knew it. She was totally comfortable with him. There was no need to worry, no need to pretend to be someone she wasn't.

CHAPTER SIXTEEN

Thus began the best week of Orla's life.

Orla woke at dawn on the Tuesday of her holiday with a glowing feeling. She felt happy. This was not a feeling Orla was used to, but the recent weeks had helped her to find the feeling again. Her physical job had improved her fitness, and her simple diet of vegetables had renewed her vitality. The pale spring light was seeping around the blind on the window, signalling the day. Orla rose slowly out of the bed and stretched like the cat she had become. She sat cross-legged on the floor and meditated for fifteen minutes. Orla had found meditation very difficult to start with; her mind was always racing on like a greyhound out of a trap, thoughts whizzing past her. She was gradually learning to calm her mind and let these thoughts float away, however. She went deeper, concentrating on the image of a lotus flower she held in her mind, aware of her breathing, finally seeing deep blackness. As usual, an image of Elijah formed itself, and then one of Nathaniel. She tried unsuccessfully to dismiss them. Orla opened her eyes and ceased trying to meditate.

She wondered if it was her unconscious trying to tell her something. She still couldn't seem to achieve the nothingness of the Buddhists. The thought came that she was as bad at meditating as she was at everything else, but she checked her negative thought, knowing that she had made some real progress. Her preoccupation with men and love would mean she would never be a true Buddhist. She wondered how it was possible to let it go. How did the Dalai Lama manage? He must be made of different stuff from Orla.

She sighed at her weakness and began her yoga routine, which she could just about manage on the tiny floor space next to the bed. Orla was better at yoga than meditation, and she enjoyed the stretches her body made and the relaxed rhythm of the movements. Feeling better, she stood up and looked down at her naked body. Her abdomen was definitely flatter than it had been, and her legs and arms had developed small, hard muscles. Her skin was too pale for Orla's liking, as it had seen so little sun over the winter. Her body was speckled with moles and freckles—so much so that a doctor had told her she shouldn't go out in the sun due to danger of cancer. Orla had ignored the advice. She loved the sun. Everything you loved wasn't allowed. Orla silently damned her Scottish colouring. She imagined herself as a dark Italian girl with sleek black hair and nut-brown skin: full of mystery. Orla didn't think anyone glamorous had ever been Scottish. She couldn't think of anyone anyway.

Today was the day Elijah was coming.

It was funny how different it felt from when Nathaniel came. She felt no sense of worry or stress. It was just perfectly natural. Elijah was her friend, and he would like her whatever she was wearing, whether she had makeup on or not. She felt no need to make an effort. Orla padded to the kitchen in her bathrobe and bare feet and boiled herself two eggs. She put on the radio and listened to the doom Radio 4 had to offer—always bad news. The presenters always managed to irritate her somehow, and so did the state of the human race. She shut it off after a few minutes, preferring the silence. She could just make out the birds singing in the garden and the comforting coo of the two turtledoves that had taken residence in the eaves. Grimalkin made a rare appearance, looking up at her with a request for food in his eyes. She fed him from the huge bag of cat food she had got on offer and admired him as he ate. Orla was toying with the idea of getting a dog. She enjoyed the company of animals and had found them much more peaceable than humans.

Still no Elijah.

Orla wondered if Elijah's idea of bright and early was different from hers. Orla ran the bath in her usual leisurely style and read *Wuthering Heights* while she waited for it to fill. Orla did make some concessions to Elijah's visit. She used her most expensive bath oils and luxurious hair treatments she had left over from many Christmases ago. She lay in the bath as usual for too long, feeling a wonderful sense of calm and well-being. Well pleased with the feel of her skin and her fragrance, she towelled herself dry and applied her body butter. Orla danced around the bedroom while she waited for it to dry, imagining herself waltzing with a prince in Vienna. She laughed at herself.

"You will never grow up, Orla," she scolded out loud. But she didn't really care. Orla did not want to grow up, did not want to be like other people. She had learned to love herself again in her little world now that she was out of the critical gaze of others. She was happy with herself and with her friendship with Elijah, who never criticised her. She didn't need other people.

Still no Elijah.

Orla threw on her jeans and an old fleece with thick walking socks. She pulled on her Wellingtons by the kitchen door and went out to the garden. She wasn't concerned. He would come when he came. She began weeding the vegetable patch, feeling sorry for the little weeds that had to die when they were just starting out to make way for the superior vegetables. Orla worked methodically, singing to herself as she worked. She became aware of somebody watching her…an animal instinct. She looked up and there he was: Elijah. She straightened up and looked at him, her face involuntarily broadening into a wide smile. He was more beautiful than she remembered.

He seemed to have grown even taller—definitely over six feet now—and he was broader than she remembered. Within moments, they were hugging each other. She could feel his arms right around her as she was buried in his chest. He was almost lifting her off the ground. They stayed like this for many minutes. It had been totally instinctive, no thought involved. Eventually, she pulled away.

"Coffee?" she inquired, looking up into his perfectly blue eyes.

"Yes," he replied with a huge smile. "I just need to get something from my bike."

He set off at a jog around the side of the house. Orla walked to the back door of the house and began making coffee in the filter machine. Her face seemed fixed with a permanent, idiotic smile.

She felt his presence behind her and turned to see Elijah in the doorway holding out something to her.

"I got you this, seeing as you are such a drunk," he said, grinning at her.

"Oh, where did you get it? You didn't steal it," Orla squeaked in mock shock.

"Nah, it's from my dad's collection. He won't miss it. He's got loads."

Orla took it from him and looked at the label. It was a reserve Rioja—just exactly what she liked.

They stood beaming at each other for some moments, and then he took a step towards her and held her face between his hands. He kissed her very gently on the lips. Orla backed away in surprise and said quietly, "I think we should drink the coffee." She had not expected him to be so physical, at least not so soon, and she felt slightly rattled. She had that out-of-control feeling. It was delicious, but she was also scared of it. Half of her wanted her relationship with Elijah to stay as a friendship, to be safe, not to go into the danger zone. She was still smarting from the Nathaniel experience.

Elijah appeared unconcerned as ever. He grabbed the coffee and sat at the kitchen table, lounging across the chair. He seemed to take up most of the room. Orla sat opposite him. She could not stop smiling at him in spite of her fears. They drank the coffee and talked of mundanities. He told her about his holidays at the base and how dull it was, made her laugh with stories of his aunt's eccentricities and how he played tricks on her. They laughed easily together, and Orla forgot her uneasiness. She showed him the house, such as it was, and the garden. He looked intently at everything with great interest and made all the right noises about how he liked it all. Then, at Orla's suggestion, they went on a walk over the stubble fields, arm in arm. It was a perfectly still afternoon with cold spring sunshine. Everything seemed brighter. The earth was beginning to wake up. Orla could feel it. There were still snowdrops under the trees, and the daffodils were out at the roadside. They had a perfect afternoon.

On their return to the house, Elijah announced that he needed to leave but looked into her eyes and said, "Can I come back tomorrow?"

Orla laughed, and for the second time that afternoon she was reminded of his youth. He was looking at her plaintively, asking to be allowed to do something.

"You mean can you come and play tomorrow? Yes, of course you can!"

This time it was she who leaned forward to kiss him. She meant it as a peck on the cheek, but he turned his face so his mouth was covering hers. They were locked in a kiss for several minutes. His lips tasted incredibly soft as his mouth moved over hers instinctively, with more skill than she had envisioned. He seemed totally in charge of her, and this time she did not resist but gave herself up to the moment. To Orla, they seemed to be kissing forever. Eventually, he pulled away, smiled widely, and left without saying anything.

Orla stood in the kitchen as if a dream had happened. She was stunned and delighted all at once. Her fears had completely gone. They had kissed. It had felt totally right to her. Later that evening, she opened the wine and enjoyed a glass. It tasted as perfect as the afternoon had been.

Orla felt she was glowing from deep inside. She knew anyone looking at her would instantly know she was in love.

But nobody was looking at her.

The following day, Orla was baking bread in the kitchen, pummelling the dough and enjoying the rhythmic exercise of her fingers. Elijah arrived unannounced, knocking at the door.

Today he was full of energy and fun.

"Let's go out somewhere. In your car. The coast. We'll go to the coast."

Orla loved the sea. They always seemed to chime together in tune.

"What if someone sees us?" worried Orla.

"They won't."

"But the coast is popular on sunny days. Someone from school might see. Dunwich is quieter."

"Dunwich it is then."

They set off in Orla's red Mini. Orla wore a summer-print dress, slightly too summery for the season, with gold-trimmed flip-flops and a fluffy pink mohair wrap to keep her warm. She applied light makeup and felt good. She was dressed for fun rather than any serious walking. Elijah had on his usual trainers, jeans, and T-shirt and refused to wear a jacket despite Orla's protestations that the coast would be cold. In fact, it wasn't cold at all. The weather bloomed into warm sunshine, conspiring with them against the world. They walked hand in hand along the pebbly beach, staring out to sea, sometimes talking and laughing, sometimes in companionable silence. They drank tea and fed each other chips in the little cafe. Then they just sat on the pebbles on a plaid blanket, holding hands and enjoying the sensation of being with each other.

Another perfect day.

When they got back to Orla's cottage, she made coffee, and they sat entwined around each other on the one comfortable chair in front of the Aga.

Elijah said, "I want to spend the whole night with you."

Orla looked him in the eyes and giggled. "Does that mean what I think it does?"

"Yes," Elijah replied, looking at her in that direct, searching way that she could not resist.

"We can't," stated Orla flatly.

"Why?"

"You know why. You're too young. You should have a normal girlfriend your own age and do all that with her. Like normal people."

"I want you."

Orla didn't say anything, but her silence told him she had given in. Elijah got his own way as usual. He took charge of the situation as ever.

"I'll come tomorrow evening. Make some excuse that I'm going to a friend's for a sleepover. We can have dinner and then spend all night together. It'll be fantastic."

He kissed her on the cheek, jumped up, and went off on his bike.

Orla felt breathless and stunned. Of course she wanted to, but she had some nerves about it. It wasn't even his age that was bothering her now. It was the memory of what had happened with Nathaniel. Of course she felt totally different with Elijah. He was totally different. Her confidence was at a low ebb. His expectations would be too high. No. She dismissed these thoughts. It would be fine. She couldn't resist him. She gave him everything he asked. It was irresistible.

CHAPTER SEVENTEEN

The following evening, Orla felt like she was in a dream or in a film. Things flowed around her. She was calm and serene. She prepared a rabbit stew with the leftover poached rabbit she had frozen earlier in the week and put some potatoes in to roast. Orla didn't really know what Elijah liked to eat, so she guessed. She decided on chocolate mousse for dessert and then some cheeses with her homemade bread. Orla was a simple, rustic cook, but she knew how to make things taste good. Orla laid the table as if she were in a restaurant, with a white linen tablecloth and her best cutlery and glassware. She surveyed her handiwork with pride. She realised that she had never had a man round to dinner like this—not ever. Orla mused that she would have made someone a very good wife. She sighed and dismissed the thought.

For once, she decided to make an effort with her appearance for Elijah. Up to now she had always stayed casual. While the dinner bubbled away, she bathed and anointed herself with many creams and potions. As her hands smoothed the lotions over her body, she admired the smoothness of her skin and her small, hard muscles. The little hairs on her arms had turned white blond due to her spending so much time outdoors. She blow-dried her hair using the round brush to make it bouffant, deciding against spray, as it would make it feel stiff. Orla loved the feel of its softness between her fingers. She applied full makeup, pleased with the way the foundation covered all her tiny skin flaws. Orla decided on black lace lingerie and stay-up stockings. She pulled on a black cocktail dress she had only worn once before and finished off with impossibly high black stilettos she could barely walk in. She tried to admire herself in the tiny mirror but could only see parts of herself at any one time. She was pleased with her face anyway. Orla was surprised at how glamorous she looked. She sprayed herself in too much perfume and tottered back to the kitchen. She was beginning to feel excited, elated even. She uncorked the wine and looked around for something else to do. There was nothing. She just had to wait. Orla settled in the armchair and began to read a poetry anthology she had not looked at for years. It was Seamus Heaney, whom she had studied at school and who had remained a favourite ever since. She savoured his skill with words, the sensuous earthiness of them. She began to read out loud to better enjoy the sounds. As she read, she slowly became aware of a presence. Elijah was standing in front of her. He had come in soundlessly while she was reading.

"Oh!" Orla squeaked in surprise and felt herself go pink, embarrassed to have been caught reading poetry so fervently. She was painfully aware from teaching that poetry was not considered to be cool. But Elijah was not concerned. He was smiling at her with an intensity she had not seen before. He took the book from her and read the poem she had been reading.

"It sounded amazing. Who is it? I love the way you speak. It's like you're English but there's something else in the background. It's so sexy."

Orla giggled. Elijah always made her giggle.

"It's Heaney. He's Irish. The greatest living poet in my view. And me. Well, it's Scots you can hear in the back of my accent. I've lived in England so long it's almost gone."

She stood up to meet him, and he enfolded her in his arms for what seemed like a long time. He kissed the nape of her neck and whispered, "You look totally amazing. I've never seen you with your hair down before."

He took a lock of hair in his fingers and twisted it. She pulled away, feeling heady with the intensity of her feelings. Orla explained about the dinner. They sat down to eat, and Orla recovered some sense of normality over the food. She noticed that he had impeccable table manners, perhaps a benefit of a military family. Elijah regaled her with stories of his home life on the base: escapades with the other children, tales of his crazy aunt who seemed to be looking after him very ineffectually, music and computer games he liked. Orla was uncharacteristically quiet, just drinking him in, still amazed he was there at all, this beautiful, unearthly being in her house who seemed to like her as much as she liked him. She was permanently surprised that he was here at all. They finally got to the cheese and coffee. By this time, Orla began to feel too hot and heady. It was the wine, she told herself…but it wasn't. It was the thought of what was to come. Her elation had become mixed with trepidation, and irrational fears were surfacing within her. Orla excused herself, saying she needed air, and went to sit on the bench in the garden. Elijah followed her out soon after and sat beside her. He put his lips against her hair and whispered in her ear.

"What's wrong?"

"Nothing. Everything. I don't know. I feel nervous. What you expect. It won't be like you imagine."

"No, it will be better." He laughed briefly.

Orla turned to face him and found herself losing herself in his eyes as usual. She could not resist them; they banished any vestiges of better judgement she might have had.

She decided on the direct approach. "What do you know about sex?"

"Everything."

"Oh, come on." She glared at him in frustration.

"OK. Well I've seen it in films and on the Internet." He hesitated. "I've watched porn on the Internet…I hope you don't disapprove."

"No, I don't disapprove. It's perfectly natural to be interested. I wish there had been all that stuff when I was young. I didn't know anything. But the fact remains that real sex isn't like that. I worry you will be disappointed."

"I know that. I am not an idiot. I want you. It will be fine."

"I can't teach you, if that's what you want. I am not experienced. I was married once, but it was a very long time ago. I don't think I was ever very good at it."

He sighed heavily. "You are overthinking it all. Stop worrying. Just relax and go with what you want."

She smiled and turned back towards him. He was right, of course. He seemed to understand her more than she did. He seemed to have knowledge beyond his years. How could he be like that? She moved her face closer to his and cupped his face in her hands. He kissed her on the mouth, a kiss that seemed to go on into eternity, a kiss that she did not want to stop. She forgot her worries with the kiss; nothing mattered anymore. She did not know how they got to the bedroom, but they did. Orla was lying on the bed with the weight of Elijah on top of her. They were endlessly kissing each other. Orla could not remember ever enjoying kissing someone as much as this. Their mouths just seemed to fit together. Elijah stopped and smiled down at her.

"You are OK now, aren't you?" he questioned.

Her smile was answer enough. He fingered the zip at the back of her dress, and she turned over to give better access. He unzipped her and slipped her dress down, taking it right over her feet.

Orla turned over to face him again. She giggled as his eyes lit up with delight at the sight of her breasts in the expensive, seldom-worn bra. He began to kiss her neck, working his way down to the crevice between her breasts. He undid the clasp of her bra and removed the garment from her. He stopped still and stared at her breasts as if they were rare gems he had come across. He began kneading one of them between his fingers, then caressing, then kissing her nipple and licking it with his tongue. A thought of surprise passed through Orla at how confident he was. He certainly had watched a lot of films. She had almost stopped thinking, given herself up to the body, but not quite.

She felt his tongue edge its way down to her navel, encircling the hole repeatedly with his tongue. He gave out a noise that was like some primal animal and removed his own clothes in a fast frenzy. Then he was back at her lips, smothering her in kisses. He entered her quickly, probing her without difficulty. She opened herself wide to receive him, and this time there was no pain. She was ready…more than ready. After some brief thrusts, it was over for him, and he collapsed on top of her, pink with frustration. She laughed at the situation and kissed him on the forehead gently, giving words of comfort.

"It's just because it's the first time. It will last longer next time. Stay inside me."

So he did, and after a short while they tried again, and it did last longer, and it was better. It was slow and gentle. Orla didn't orgasm, but she felt warm and fuzzy and very loved. Elijah lay back on the bed next to her breathing heavily.

"Are you OK?" Orla asked simply.

"I am more than OK," he replied, laughing gently. "I feel amazing."

They fell asleep, contentedly wrapped around each other, fitting together.

The week continued in this vein. Elijah came to see Orla every day. They ate, they drank wine, they walked, they made love, exploring each other, learning what the other one liked, giving each other pleasure. Elijah learned fast, and Orla felt totally relaxed with him; it was perhaps the only time she had felt this in her entire life. It was as if they were in a dream of love, in the Garden of Eden.

CHAPTER EIGHTEEN

The perfect week was over too quickly. Elijah returned to school, and Orla to her job and her garden. The warmth stayed with her, and she glided through her tasks with a newfound serenity. Happiness and contentment had almost become hers. She was becoming more confident in other aspects of her life. Tentatively, she began to imagine new careers, new horizons. They kept up communication through Facebook and texts. It was enough to keep Orla buoyant, and she dared to imagine the experience could be repeated in the next holiday. Summer was not very far away.

But the snake had crept into the garden. One day, the messages from Elijah just stopped. Orla was puzzled. There had been no warning, no argument. It was the beginning of June, and the garden was bursting with life, flowers about to blossom, bees buzzing about their business. Summer was waiting. Orla was waiting. She let a week slip by and then another one. Unease began to return—a feeling of dread in the pit of her stomach. What had happened? She messaged him with no response. The following day, she did it again. No response. And again. And again. It was like his earlier messages to her. The tables had turned. Why was he ignoring her? She didn't know what to do. She couldn't believe it had happened again. Surely he wouldn't do what Nathaniel had done?

Orla began to wilt as she carried out her daily tasks. The sense of despair she had felt before didn't quite return. After all, she was glad it had happened, that she had had the experience. Even if it was never repeated, she had known true joy and what she had thought was love. It was enough. There was also the part of herself that thought he would return, that part that wouldn't quite give up hope. It kept her going; the tiny flame burning within, almost in danger of blowing out but never quite doing so. The flame was fanned by Orla's dreams, in which Elijah continued to come to her, continued to smile at her, continued to kiss her. The flame kept Orla going through the early summer days. She told herself to keep busy, and she did. Orla enlarged the vegetable patch, planting out tomato plants, chillies, and strawberries. She repainted the kitchen in a brilliant white and cleared out her cupboards. She kept faith. Orla prayed and lit candles, asking God to send love back to her.

She refused to let the darkness envelop her, not again.

One Friday morning in late June, Orla was lying in bed. She had had a restless sleep with disturbing dreams. As she lay in the dawn light, she felt a shiver move across her, like icy fingers down her back, a terrible coldness. It reminded Orla of that phrase—that someone has walked across your grave. She felt rattled. She was sensitive to things—atmospheres of places, feelings of people. Orla knew it meant something. But what? She roused herself, put on her fluffy bathrobe, and made herself coffee. She sat in the garden to drink it in the cold morning light, unconcerned that she was half dressed. Orla had never been concerned with respectability or what people thought. The only person who could see her anyway would be Frank, and he would be long gone either at work or out shooting something. He was an early riser.

Unexpectedly, there was a loud rap on the door. Orla jumped. There was another rap and then another—loud, cold, and commanding. Orla went to the door in dread. She just knew this was no ordinary visitor. She opened the door to see two people standing there. The woman had to be the ugliest person Orla could ever remember seeing. She was short, squat, and incredibly obese. She was wearing black trousers, white socks, and flat black slip-on shoes, and her feet seemed to sort of splay out, reminding Orla of a penguin. She was wearing a stained red Mac. Orla raised her eyes to the woman's face. The eyes were a pale, watery brown, and she had nondescript mousy hair, which had maybe originally have been cut short but was now growing unkempt. Orla felt herself physically recoil from the ugliness before her. The man with the woman was nondescript: greying, fifties, average height, average everything—like millions of others. The two introduced themselves as police officers and gave her names, which she would not recall. Things then happened as if in a dream. Orla heard words but could not make sense of them—references to Northwold School, children, Elijah, inciting a child to sexual activity…Orla was arrested, read her rights, told to get dressed. To Orla's disgust, the woman watched her intently as she took off her robe and put on jeans and a sweater. This was how she got her kicks, apparently. Orla was told not to wear a belt and not to bring anything. They took her laptop and her Blackberry, and she was led to the unmarked car. All the while, Orla felt numb. Orla felt nothing. Orla was not really there. Part of her had been expecting this moment all along. She had always known it was a risk. Yet she had given in to her feelings anyway, allowed herself a brief happiness. Images of prison flashed through her mind. She would be bullied, nobody would like her, the food would be terrible, the cells stark, the guards cold and sneering. It would be just like Northwold. She would be used to it. Everything would be back to normal—unhappiness, despair, loneliness. This was Orla's normality. Orla didn't feel anything, didn't mind. She had detached from herself.

The police station was an old, stone building in the heart of town. Orla was led into the reception area. The desk sergeant, young and innocent looking, little more than a boy, looked at Orla with evident surprise. She was not the sort of person they usually saw. He asked her lots of ridiculous questions: dietary habits, religion, possibility of pregnancy…Orla answered in monotone. The pregnancy question made her start. She had used no contraception, hadn't even thought about it. The relationship had happened in a dream world where such things didn't matter. She didn't know the answer. She answered no.

Next there was the cell. Orla was locked into the bare room. The walls were bare brick painted white, and there was a Crimestoppers poster asking inmates to snitch on their friends. Orla sat on a flat, seat-like object that jutted out from one of the walls. At the side Orla could see a toilet. There was nothing else. Nothing apart from an all-seeing eye: a camera from which the police could watch your every move. So they watched people go to the toilet in the cells. Orla was reminded of Orwell. She felt similar to the character in *1984*. She was Winston, adrift in a Big Brother world that she did not understand. She did not fit in, had never fitted in. But modern society would force her. She was trapped.

Bring on the rats! thought Orla.

Having nothing else to do, Orla turned to God. She prayed awkwardly, wondering what to say. She started with the Lord's Prayer and then said other half-remembered prayers from childhood. Then, more simply, she pleaded, "Help me. Help me. I don't deserve it, but help me."

After what seemed like an interminable amount of time, the door opened, and she was taken for interview. At first, Orla was left alone with the duty solicitor. He was yet another nondescript male: in his fifties, greying, slightly overweight, Northern Irish accent. He told her what was going to happen, and he affected affability. Orla wondered about all of these people: how they felt inside. Police officers, solicitors, teachers: they felt themselves above others—that they had the right to tell others what to do, to set themselves above. They were better, superior. What gave them the right to feel like that? Did it give them a thrill? Though in one of these professions, she had never felt like that, had never felt superior to anyone. There were times when she had hated her job so much that she had become envious of refuse collectors, waiters, postal workers…anyone…everyone.

So the arresting officer came in, the same woman who had been at the house. Orla felt herself recoil as if from an insect or some repulsive alien creature. The solicitor told her to answer "no comment" to everything. So she did. The questions came thick and fast, like swords stabbing into her over and over. The first sentence: "We have had a disclosure from Elijah Haynes."

He had betrayed her. From his own lips. Whatever Orla had expected, it wasn't that he would deliberately get her into trouble. Coldness enveloped her. It was too horrible to contemplate.

The officer read out the messages between her and Elijah from Facebook, asking her to comment on each one. It became apparent to Orla that the messages had been doctored—very cleverly, as it happened. Most of Elijah's were missing, except when he had said something negative or bad tempered. Orla's were not complete either. Anything caring, loving, or merely chatty had been excised. The ones left were the flirtatious ones and then the sad ones, asking him what had happened and where he was. In spite of her shock, some cold, logical part of her brain was still functioning—sifting the statements, assessing the damage, calculating how to get herself out of the mess with the least amount of trouble. She was surprised at the steely instinct for survival that she did not know she possessed. It did not take her long, as the statements rained down on her, to realise that there was another hand at work here. Whatever Elijah was, he was not clever enough to have engineered this or patient enough to have gone through it all. Somebody was taking a careful, calculated revenge on Orla. She was being made to look like some evil Svengali who had lured the innocent child into a trap. It didn't matter. She was the adult, and he was the minor. She would always be in the wrong, and she would not be believed. Bizarrely, she also began to realise that she was not even being accused of having sex with him. She was facing the lesser charge of inciting a minor into sexual activity. According to Elijah, he had never seen her out of school or been to her house; the relationship had been entirely conducted through Facebook. Part of Orla began to doubt her own sanity. Was she so crazy that she had imagined the whole thing? She had fabricated entire events, fabricated a whole relationship? But she knew this wasn't so. She was eccentric, she was strange, but she was not insane. Orla began to feel more and more like Winston from *1984*. Reality was whatever the authorities wanted it to be. It didn't matter what had actually happened. Orla didn't really care what happened to her. But inside was the cold reality that Elijah had betrayed her. A little voice suggested that perhaps this hadn't happened, perhaps he had been forced into it. But the cynical, harder part of herself said she was doing what she had always done: making excuses for weak, inadequate men, thinking the best of them when all the time they were only thinking of themselves. The facts seemed to speak for themselves. He had set out, coldly and calculatingly, to destroy her. Could she really believe it? Had he used her just like Nathaniel? He had seemed so much more genuine, so much more interested in her as a person. If it had all been a show, he was the best actor in England.

After an interminable amount of time, which Orla could not measure, the police officer's mouth stopped moving. She was allowed to go. Orla was released into the street with her paperwork, having been told to return in September after the police completed an examination of her computer. She realised with a sickening jolt what they were looking for: pornographic images of children. They imagined she was a paedophile—a person who spent time on the Internet looking at adults having sex with children. This was what people thought of Orla…what they would think of her. Orla had little idea of paedophilia. She did not read tabloid newspapers and was only dimly aware of the hysteria surrounding the issue. She seemed to recall a kind of mob mentality that had happened a few years ago. Images flicked through Orla's mind of what could happen: her house would be firebombed, graffiti daubed on her walls, she would be made homeless, an outcast. The pitchforks would come for her. There were no conditions on her bail. She was just released. Orla didn't know why they hadn't just charged her there and then. Later, she would come to realise they did not have enough evidence. The flirty, affectionate messages were not really sufficient. They would have to prove intent to have sex with Elijah.

Orla blinked in the sunshine of the street and wondered what to do. She had no money in her pocket and no phone. She hadn't anyone she could phone anyway. Orla recognised the hard fact that she was all alone with her problem. She would not be able to tell her elderly parents. They would be horrified, judgemental. They would not take her side. She felt as outcast from her family as she did from everyone else. She walked out onto the road out of town with purposeful steps. She hitchhiked with a sugar beet lorry back to her village, her eyes not seeing the flat, uninteresting landscape. She noted from the window that the weather was not mirroring her disaster. There was no rain, no thunder and lightning, just a grey, overcast sky and thin light—a typical English summer day. There was no pathetic fallacy. The universe did not feel in sympathy with Orla. It was going about its business as usual, unconcerned.

Once home, Orla sank into the kitchen armchair. She considered getting drunk and rejected the idea. Instead she made some strong tea. Her body seemed to have gone into shock. She felt preternaturally alert, as if everything was heightened, as if she could hear the scratches the field mice made in the garden or the undulations of worms. A creeping feeling of dread, physical in force, appeared to have taken over her whole body, preventing her from thinking straight or doing anything. She stared straight ahead, her arms wrapped around herself, rocking herself back and forward in a steady rhythm. She stayed like this all day and all night.

Sleep would not come.

CHAPTER NINETEEN

The following morning, dawn seeped into the kitchen, soaking Orla in a thin light. She rose and decided it was time for action. Orla splashed her face with water from the tap and felt slightly more alive. She went out into the garden and looked at her plants. The little safe world she had constructed was shattered. The police had broken it, just like they had broken her life with Oriel all those years ago.

Oriel.

She needed help.

She needed to run. She did not know who to turn to. Orla thought of Nathaniel. The brick wall. No. He had ignored her for weeks. Something as wild as Orla could not contaminate his hygienic, anodyne, perfect world.

Oriel.

Oriel was not easily surprised. She hadn't seen him for over a decade, but she had his Facebook contact information. Except she had no computer. The police had taken it. This problem was easily remedied.

Orla drove to the nearest big supermarket in town and parked at an angle in the car park. She realised she must look a fright with her unbrushed hair and crumpled clothes.

She didn't care.

She wandered the aisles until she happened on the electronic goods section. Luckily, there were some cheap, basic laptops. She selected one at random and paid for it by credit card. The assistant looked at her with quizzical eyes, wondering what her story was. Orla smiled at her with a false brightness she had perfected at work. She drove back to her village imprecisely, bouncing the car off pavements at points and nearly toppling a cyclist. She had always been an incredibly bad driver. Now she was virtually taking a deliberate pleasure in it.

She didn't care.

Orla was not much concerned about any more things happening to her. It seemed like things couldn't possibly get any worse. Back at her cottage, she managed to set up the computer and connect it to the broadband. She mused that usually she would've found such a technical thing incredibly difficult and would've needed to ask someone else for help. Now she seemed able to do things, to be practical. Something cold and logical inside her had taken over and was guiding her, willing her to survive. The old Orla had retreated, didn't care if she lived, didn't think she had anything to live for. She felt like she was someone else—someone capable. She logged on to Facebook and found Oriel's page. She messaged him, "Oriel. It's Orla. I am in big trouble. I need to run. Can I run to Jamaica? Please answer me as soon as you get this."

It was a long shot, but it was her only hope. She knew she had no right to ask him. She was the one who had initiated the divorce. She had abandoned him. Yet there was no one else. She had a school friend in Brussels whom she hadn't seen for years. She could run there, but it seemed too close. He was respectable—not dodgy, not crazy. He wouldn't understand. She remembered the good times they had had in their youth, telling each other secrets curled up on cold days in the school cloakroom, hiding from the prefects who would throw them outside into the snow. He had got away, made a go of his life. He was something important in the European Union. Orla was happy for him. She could not inflict her disastrous self upon him. She could not contaminate him with her badness. She had cousins in Arizona. They were even more unsuitable. They were evangelical Christians. Orla had seen endless photos of them: boys with closely cropped blond hair, wearing some kind of military uniforms, staring confidently into the camera lens. Orla couldn't imagine fitting in. She had always had a strange kind of fear of the United States. It wasn't the place for her. She could not contaminate her clean-living cousins either.

Nathaniel.

Her thoughts returned to him. In spite of the way he had treated her, she still could not feel anything but warmth for him. She wondered if she dared to contact him, to tell him what had happened. In a romantic film, he would have helped her. Orla imagined turning up at his house. It would be easy to find the address on the Internet. She would fall on his mercy. He would be kind and think of a plan. But Orla was not living inside a romantic comedy where everything always turned out fine in the end. She envisioned the more likely scenario: she would turn up at his house, he would shout, his wife would appear behind him, they would slam the door in her face. She would be left standing destitute in the street. No. No Nathaniel. There was only Oriel. Nobody else left. It saddened Orla to the marrow of her bones that in her whole life she had made no friends, only work colleagues who dropped her as soon as things weren't rosy.

She was alone. She had been alone for years. She had never got used to it.

Orla lay on her bed and slept fitfully, waiting and hoping that Oriel would answer her message. On the outside, he pretended to be hard and tough—the criminal, the dealer, the man about town. Inside, Orla knew he wasn't like that. He was soft and damaged, broken, like a fledgling bird fallen from the nest. His face drifted into her mind, and she remembered his smell, his hard body she had enjoyed so much. She wished she was still in his flat in Edinburgh, in his bed, that her whole adult life hadn't happened to her. It had been so grey, so pointless, so empty. Orla realised too late that it was relationships that mattered, finding people to love who loved you in return. Her career had been a shell. She felt the feminists had lied to her, betrayed her. She would have been happier married to some ordinary guy, with a house full of noisy kids, barefoot in the kitchen. It couldn't have been worse than those dead, unappreciated years at Northwold, a servant to the nouveau riche.

After a few hours of this, she padded into the kitchen and checked the computer. There was no reply from Oriel. She typed "female sex offender" into Google and read some articles. As she flipped between websites, her feeling of cold dread increased. She could wind up going to prison for years. Orla also found that she was not alone. There were endless American articles about teachers and teenage boys. In the photos, they all looked amazingly normal. Orla wondered what their feelings had been. There was even a website in Texas called Sexiest Female Sex Offenders. Obviously some people were not taking it seriously. She read and read and absorbed the information quickly. The upshot seemed to be that in the past nobody much bothered about women in this kind of situation, but now the PC age had dawned, Orla was likely to get as heavy a sentence as a man. The male convicted sex offenders stared out of the computer at her: often heavyset, jowly, threatening. Orla felt herself one of them. Little Orla, who had never previously committed any crime. Orla, who would capture flies and spiders in glasses and take them outside rather than kill them. Orla, who had always had time for everyone and had listened to everyone's problems. Orla, who had put others before herself all her life. She was reduced to this. She was a criminal, a pervert. She kept reading. She found a table of ages of consent in different countries. Amazingly, she discovered that in some countries he would have been of age: Spain, Italy, even France. How strange that they should be the countries she loved the most, the countries that understand love. Orla closed the laptop and sat with her head in her hands. Images of her forthcoming trial flashed through her head. She imagined judgemental faces, salacious newspaper headlines, aggressive reporters, and cameramen baying for blood. She would be a pariah.

Orla fetched herself a glass of water and drank deeply. She tried to meditate and failed. She couldn't settle to anything. She paced about the cottage and garden, clasping and unclasping her hands, talking to herself, trying desperately to free her mind of clutter and think logically. After a few hours, she logged back on to Facebook. There was a message from Oriel: "Hey baby what's up? Don't tell me my angel Orla had the Feds on her case. Run to me any time."

Orla laughed with relief at the lightness of the tone and his apparent unconcern. Nothing shocked Oriel. He wasn't online, but she messaged back, "I want to come to Jamaica as soon as possible. I need to hide out. I need your address. Please."

Orla felt slightly relieved. Maybe he would help her. Maybe escape was possible. She returned to lie on the bed, and this time she actually slept for a few hours. On return to the kitchen, she logged on to Facebook with some hope in her heart. Oriel had replied briefly with the address of a bar in Ocho Rios called Coconuts, which he said he was managing for a friend and where he had a room above. It was typical Oriel: disorganised, rough round the edges, but managing to keep afloat. Tears seeped out as she wished she had stayed with him, had not listened to her uptight, disapproving parents and friends. Managing a bar in Jamaica sounded like a better deal than teaching at Northwold.

She imagined the children they could have had: beautiful, dark-skinned girls with wild hair and big eyes. She imagined herself, happy and fulfilled, cooking jerk chicken in the kitchen, joking with the customers, dancing in the evening to reggae, waking every day to glorious sunshine. It could have been wonderful. Orla pulled herself together and wrote down the address on a piece of paper. She replied simply, "I am coming."

Then she proceeded to delete all of her messages. She removed everything that had ever been there. It took over an hour. Then she changed her password and deleted her account. She closed all her email accounts as well.

Orla did not exist.

She had no idea how the police operated, whether they would try to find her or if she wasn't worth it. She knew they had her laptop, so her Facebook account could have been used as evidence. There was nothing else incriminating on it. She remembered she had saved lots of photos of Nathaniel from his Facebook page. She would miss looking at them. She didn't need any photos of Elijah; he was already in her head.

She had virtually nothing in her bank account, so she bought the ticket with her credit card online. She knew this was not what proper criminals would do. It could be traced. But maybe they wouldn't.

She was running away.

CHAPTER TWENTY

Orla had a day before the flight left. Bizarrely, the thought of action had given her a new lease on life. She felt energised—she was doing something. She was running away. Running away! Whatever fate awaited her in Jamaica, it was better than staying here and waiting for the inevitable outcome. Orla was a fugitive from justice. She reflected that in her youth she would have relished the wildness of it. She had always loved the sense of being in a film, had sought out unusual experiences and people deliberately. But something had changed within her over the years. She was much more wary, more fearful, more worried about the darkness in the world, which waited to pounce on her. Part of her still wanted to stay in the cottage that had been her protection for so long. There was no protection any longer. She wasn't safe here anymore. Big Brother was coming to get her.

Orla felt a strange need to clean the house, so she scrubbed it all over with bleach solution. She threw some clothes virtually at random into that battered leather case she had bought in an overpriced antique shop on the Suffolk coast. She had loved the old travel labels that festooned it, and she liked to imagine it had belonged to a famous actor who travelled the globe playing Shakespearean characters in the theatres of the world. She was leaving most of her winter things behind. She wouldn't need to dress for the cold in Jamaica. Orla had never been to the Caribbean and didn't really know what to expect, but she was pretty sure it would be hot. She was too wound up to eat. When she had finished her brief preparations, she lay on the bed and waited for the next day to come. She slept surprisingly deeply. In her dreams, the faces of Elijah, Oriel, and Nathaniel appeared and disappeared, reforming and coalescing until she didn't know which one was which. She didn't trust any of them. But she had to.

The sun bored in through the window, easily outwitting the thin curtains. It was a beautiful summer day. Orla decided it was a good omen. She dragged her suitcase to the door and rammed it into the back seat of her Mini. She locked the door of the cottage, kissed it good-bye, and put the key through the letterbox of next door with a note that said she was going away for a while and could he feed and look after the cat? She put a ten-pound note in for the cat food, feeling guilty that she wouldn't be back. Apart from this note, Orla told no one of her departure. She didn't really feel that anyone would miss her. Orla drove the car to the station and abandoned it there. She didn't pay. She wouldn't be back for it. She negotiated the train to Cambridge and then to London, and then she found the train to the airport. The journey passed in a blur of people and elbows and rush and heat. Orla had always felt strange in London. The people all rushed around with a sense of purpose, and they didn't chat to each other like country souls. It unnerved her; she always seemed to be in somebody's way, trying to work out which platform to get on and off at and which way to go. She had been a rural girl for so long that she had forgotten the hang of the city. She had a poor sense of direction and felt constant panic that she would go the wrong way and miss the flight. After London, the airport had an air of calm. It was big and airy and made Orla feel like she was in the future. She enjoyed the automated walkway where you were conveyed to your terminal, though she couldn't see how it was any quicker or more efficient than walking. Finally, she made it to the aeroplane. It was full of holiday makers in good moods. The journey seemed to go on for eternity. Orla had never been on a flight for this long before. She remembered that Oriel had told her that he had been sent on a plane to Britain at the age of fourteen, sent by his mother for a better life. He had turned up in Manchester to stay with relatives he had never met with a naïve hope of becoming a doctor like his mother wanted. It must have been so strange to him.

As the plane touched down in Montego Bay, she felt dread and elation in equal measure. She was on the run. Maybe they would look for her. Maybe not. She supposed they had bigger fish to fry, but you never knew. She hoped they would never find her. Orla was finally having an adventure. She splurged all of her remaining cash on a taxi to Ocho Rios. If things didn't work out, she was now penniless in a strange country. The driver was old and friendly, pointing out landmarks and attractions and asking her all about herself. He seemed particularly proud of the home for girls who had got pregnant while of school age. He thought she was a nice, churchgoing girl. Orla laughed at the idea. She had been that once, a very long time ago. She felt a growing elation at the sense of a new start.

Fuck you, Nathaniel, she shouted internally. *You might be a fancy corporate lawyer, but I am having a new life in Jamaica. And fuck you, Elijah, you lying slimeball.*

Orla surprised herself at the vehemence of her thoughts. She knew she was insane to think of Oriel as her knight in shining armour. He had never been that. But he was all she had at the moment.

Orla calmed herself by looking out of the window at the suburbs of Montego Bay. It was much more sophisticated than she had imagined, with lots of traffic and endless neat, detached houses. There were men everywhere, walking, lounging on corners, thronging through the streets. The driver explained that there was a political meeting going on. Orla felt vaguely threatened by the atmosphere, but she felt safe with the grandfatherly driver. The taxi was modern and air conditioned, protecting Orla from the heat outside. It was all very different from what she had expected. Eventually, they were out of the city and ribboning through the countryside at great speed. Now there was little traffic. Orla marvelled at the greenery. Everything seemed brighter and bolder, and the sun was brighter than she had ever seen when she took off her sunglasses to peer at the roadside restaurants with their painted signs for jerk chicken and their tumbles of smiling children.

Orla wondered what the trees were they were passing. She could see green hills in the distance. She liked the countryside so much better than the city. This was much more the Jamaica she had expected.

Eventually, the sun began to fall over the horizon, and the taxi pulled up outside Coconuts Bar. The town was nothing impressive, just a collection of shops, bars, and houses that looked like they had been thrown down by the hand of a giant, higgledy piggledy, with no thought for order or design. The bar, slap bang in the middle of the main street, looked like it catered to tourists, with a thatched roof and wooden pillars, hoardings advertising meals and cocktails, and hand-painted signs. Orla paid the taxi driver, thanked him, and lugged her case into the bar's interior. She now felt a sense of panic that she had to face Oriel. There was a young girl tending the bar who looked barely out of her teens. She was wearing white shorts, flip-flops, and an orange T-shirt, with her hair scraped back into a simple bun. She looked surprised at the advent of Orla but smiled encouragingly at her.

"I've come to see Oriel," Orla said and then stopped nervously. She looked around and couldn't see him anywhere. There were a couple of locals playing pool and a young tourist couple eating. It was pretty quiet.

The bar girl laughed and smiled broadly. "You are Orla!" She grinned.

"Yes."

Orla was relieved that at least she was expected.

The girl disappeared into the back, and a few moments later, Oriel appeared. He was older and more grim but just about the same. He still had his hair in long, neat dreadlocks tied behind his head. He was still wearing the heavy, gold jewellery that Orla used to hate: heavy rings and a huge medallion with Haile Selassie depicted on it. He was wearing a printed shirt, long shorts, and some very heavy-looking black trainers, which Orla surmised would be some designer brand she had never heard of.

Orla realised he must be about fifty by now, but he didn't look it. He was still as thin as ever, no sign of the paunch most men his age developed. His face was barely lined, though Orla could see some new scars had etched their way across his left cheek. He smiled at her widely and immediately, showing the gold tooth he had been so proud of. She found it hard to believe she had ever been married to him. If she had met him in the street in recent years, she would have been afraid of him, shrank from him with unease. He looked so fierce.

"Orla, my angel!"

He reached out for her, and Orla felt herself fall against him, realising that this was the first human contact she had had for weeks. She felt darkness closing in around her. She fainted.

CHAPTER TWENTY-ONE

Orla woke to find herself propped up on thick pillows in a strange bed. An elderly, skinny black man with a bald head and little brown glasses was feeling her neck with two fingers and humming to himself. She realised he must be a doctor. He had a doctor air about him. He smiled benignly at Orla and retreated outside the room to talk to someone.

Orla noted that everyone in Jamaica she had met so far had had a beautiful smile. She heard the doctor use the words *nervous exhaustion* and *lots of bed rest*. Orla realised that stickiness was running down her legs. She thought it must be her period, but when she checked she found it was her own internal juices. This meant she had had sex recently. Very recently. Oriel. He must have done it while she was asleep. She had no memory of it. She realised she didn't actually mind. It meant he still found her desirable. This could only be a good thing. Orla also realised that most women would consider this rape. Orla was unusual. This was why she got into trouble. She was different from other women. Different from everyone. She felt suddenly safe and warm in the room. It had old, dark, wooden furniture and plain white sheets. The walls were busy, littered with framed photos of Oriel in various incarnations of himself. There were some of various children laughing into the camera. Orla couldn't work out if they were the same ones at different ages or different ones. There was a huge gold crucifix opposite the bed with rosary beads draped over it. It was very like his bedroom in the flat in Edinburgh. He hadn't changed. She laughed about all the photos of himself. So vain! Oriel could not really love a woman because he was too in love with himself. She didn't mind. Men were usually arrogant. It was how things were.

The next few weeks passed in a kind of hazy dream. Orla was ordered to stay in bed for the first week. Oriel brought her food from the kitchen and fed her like a baby. At first, it was cornmeal porridge only, which Oriel fed her with a spoon. From the bar he brought her fashion magazines and dog-eared paperbacks to read. She was exposed to female worlds in these magazines she had forgotten existed. She liked the perfume ads the best—perfect, glamorous women with flawless skin and expensive jewels and clothes. Orla would have liked to be in that world. She read endless articles about how to improve your relationship, how to have a better sex life, how to get a man, how to keep a man, how to get rid of a man, how to tell if your man is having an affair. According to these publications, women's lives revolved around men. Perhaps, thought Orla, she should have paid more attention to such advice. She wasn't convinced that the advice was actually worth anything though. She lost herself in the melodramatic romances of the paperbacks and the excitement and violence of the thrillers. The bar had air conditioning, so the whirr of it kept Orla cool as she read. Oriel's idea of a nutritious diet for Orla also included Red Stripe lager, Guinness, and plenty of sensimelia tea. She was kept in a permanent daze from this combination, but it was a pleasant one, and she felt herself healing; slowly and bit by bit, she was putting herself back together. She was cosy in the bed, in the dark cocoon of the room, and Oriel was looking after her. Late in the evening, he would climb into bed next to her and have sex with her. She realised as she felt his weight on top of her that she did not love him anymore at all, and yet she still found the experience comforting. She did not feel a great deal and didn't enter into the proceedings with any great enthusiasm, but this small gift seemed to satisfy Oriel, who would roll off her soon enough into a deep, contented sleep. His body was thin and bony, marked with scars and lacerations from all the trouble he had been in. He had prison tattoos snaking over his arms and chest, strange symbols that Orla did not recognise; she did not really want to know what they represented. She still liked the smell of him: smoke, sweat, and something sweet and indefinable.

Orla's dreams were vivid: Nathaniel and Elijah were alternately vying for space in her mental landscape. She longed for both of them with a yearning that was exquisitely painful. Yet they had both hurt her beyond measure. They had betrayed and abandoned her. She wished she could hate them or forget them, but she couldn't. They were always recurring in her dreams and were still there in the morning, filling up her head like cotton wool until she couldn't think. The force of the images and the unpleasantness of the experiences they had given to her made her writhe and sweat in the night. Her back would arch, and she would buck with the horror of her feelings.

"Get out of my head," she would shout at them when alone. But they wouldn't get out of her head. Elijah was the most persistent. She saw him often at the edge of a wood, calling her name, beckoning her to come with him, his fingers clutching at her clothes and at her face, clawing at her. Orla was afraid of what was in the wood behind him, afraid of what he wanted to show her. Her faint voice of reason told her not to go in the wood. In the daytime, Orla tried not to remember these dreams. They were the serpent in the Garden of Eden. She must not listen to the serpent.

In the second week, Orla was allowed to get up. She wandered around the bar and then ventured as far as the beach. She would take a book, a huge straw hat, and shades and sit on a yellow beach towel and read—and stare out to sea and read again. If she concentrated hard on the words, the images of Nathaniel and Elijah receded to the corners of her brain where she felt more in control of them. The searing Jamaican sun warmed her soul, and the cold feeling of dread she had carried in her body for the last few weeks gradually receded. She felt much more confident now she was out of Britain. Nobody here knew what she had done. Nobody knew she was a bad person. She gazed up at the perfect yellow ball and felt it was God loving her, healing her, making everything right again. She prayed silently every day for forgiveness, fervently and desperately. She wasn't sure if God heard her or even if he was really there. But he was all she had.

The beach was perfect. The sand was fine and yellow, and the sea was clear azure blue. Orla became brave enough to leave her towel and wander along the shoreline. She ventured nervously into the shallows and felt the water as warm as a bath. The sound of the gently breaking waves soothed her. Orla kept apart from the tourists. They were a mixture of Jamaicans from the city and more adventurous Americans who had escaped from the all-inclusive hotels that stretched along the coast. She did not feel ready to talk to people, and she avoided their eyes.

Oriel, more confident now that she was getting better, began to disappear for days. Orla didn't mind. After all, she was used to her own company. She started to eat downstairs in the bar—jerk chicken, salt cod, fresh fish, pineapple, ackee, rice, and peas. She loved all of it. Her appetite returned with a vengeance. She had no money to pay for anything, so she helped out as much as she could. She cleared the tables and sometimes took orders. She mopped the floor and learned how to pour drinks and make cocktails. She enjoyed it. She began to feel almost capable, skilful. Orla wondered if Oriel would let her work in the kitchen and prepare the food. She would like that. She resolved to ask him when she felt stronger. The locals who frequented the bar started to smile and nod at her. They kept their distance though, and Orla noticed they were deferential to Oriel. He was the boss. Orla liked to watch them and listen to their talk. They drank little and talked lots. They got into arguments about the sport constantly showing on the TV screen and then broke often into laughter at some joke or other. Orla found them comforting.

One morning, Orla woke alone to find a small boy standing at the foot of the bed. He was almost as black as Oriel, and Orla surmised he was about eight years old. He had long dreadlocks and a wide, cheeky smile with huge white teeth standing out from the darkness of his face. He was wearing a white T-shirt, blue shorts, and plastic sandals. He was standing with his belly poking out and his hands behind his head, regarding Orla carefully. Orla was shocked to discover him in her room. After being labelled a paedophile, she was reticent with children and had avoided them on the beach.

"Hello," she ventured.

The child's smile broadened.

"Hello," he returned carefully, as if he was not used to saying this word, and then, "I am Benjamin. I am strong like a lion." His voice was high and had a singsong quality.

Orla laughed in delight at the bizarre nature of his introduction. "I am sure you are," she said. "I am Orla. I am weak like a lamb."

He laughed at her joke and climbed onto the bed. Then without warning he climbed up to Orla's face and flung his arms around her neck. Orla, though startled, hugged him back by instinct. They stayed like this for some moments before he pulled back laughing uproariously as if something incredibly funny was happening.

"You are Oriel's wife," he said, stating it as a statement rather than a question.

Orla answered as if it had been a question.

"No, I am not his wife…I am an…old friend," she said uncertainly.

"I think you are Oriel's wife because you are in Oriel's bed."

Orla reflected that there was no way to answer this, so she stayed silent.

Benjamin invited her to the beach. They sat together a few feet from the shore, and Orla read her book while Benjamin busied himself making sand castles, tunnels, moats, and various other rough-hewn edifices. Eventually, he got bored of playing and came to snuggle up beside Orla's shoulder.

"What ya doin'?" he asked as he peered into Orla's face.

"I'm reading."

"I can't read."

"But that's terrible. Don't you go to school?"

"No. I got thrown out. They don't like me there. I am bad. I don't want to learn to read. Looks boring."

Orla exhaled exasperatedly. She knew there was no point lecturing him, but she resolved to change his mind somehow. She would have to be subtle.

"So tell me all about yourself. What are you to Oriel?"

"Well, Oriel is my brethren. He kind of look out for me. My mother, she dead. Oriel just say, 'Well, he's here now. What can you do?'"

Orla felt surprised at this matter-of-fact potted history of Benjamin's short life.

Benjamin leapt up suddenly. "Come on, Orla. I am showing you special places."

And he did. Over the following week, Benjamin walked miles with her. He showed her waterfalls in the trees where they knelt down and felt the power of the water on their skin. He took her in a little boat, and they spent hours trying to catch fish, but the fish seemed too clever for them most of the time. Benjamin would dive off the boat and swim away until Orla started to worry he would drown. He seemed completely fearless. In return for sharing adventures with her, Orla told him stories. It was the first step on her literary program. She would get him interested in stories, and then maybe one day he would want to read them for himself. She started with fairy tales from her own childhood, the Brothers Grimm and *A Thousand and One Nights*, tales of the silkies from the West Coast of Scotland and Bible stories. He was particularly taken with Jonah and the whale.

"Could you really get inside a whale? I would like to do that."

"Well, I am not sure it's really possible. I mean to stay alive. It's just a story."

"But it's the Bible. The word of Jah. Rastafari!"

Orla kept quiet on this point. She knew from Oriel that she was on shaky ground to criticise the Bible. Oriel would claim himself to be a Rastafarian, but his views were elastic. It was fine to drink to excess, smoke tobacco and weed, and gamble, but he followed arcane dietary advice to the letter. Orla did not argue about the illogic of it all.

Orla liked Benjamin. He was as odd and lonely as she was.

One evening, she cornered Oriel about him. She was emboldened, as she had discovered that Benjamin slept outside, curled up with the dogs on the decking at the back of the bar. He was feral.

Oriel was instantly stroppy at the mention of him. "Keep away from him," he said. "He's not right in the head. He does all kinds of bad things. I took him into town to show him the police cells, but he doesn't listen. What can you do? The youth are wasted."

Orla knew from past experience it was best not to argue. She would have to figure out something.

So the haze continued of the beach, the sun, the beer, the rum, the sensimelia, the fresh food…until Orla felt herself almost normal. She imagined she could learn to be happy in a place like this. Nothing mattered. There was no rush, no drive to do things. People just enjoyed the simplicity of their lives. It was so different from Britain.

CHAPTER TWENTY-TWO

Happiness was always elusive for Orla. The serpent awoke and slithered from his lair into Orla's dreams. Oriel had been away for a week without explanation. She spent her days as usual reading, lying on the beach, helping in the bar, and walking with Benjamin. He had become her constant companion. The days passed peacefully without incident, and Orla felt she should be content, but there was a restlessness in her. Things still did not feel as they should.

It was late, and Orla felt a strange oppression in the air. The weather channel beamed in from the United States by satellite had predicted a hurricane on the way. Orla had never been in a hurricane and felt a sense of apprehension. There was already a wind whipping the palm trees and blowing debris down the beach. Orla closed the window of her bedroom—or, to be more precise, Oriel's bedroom—and resolved to hole up in bed for the evening. She put some gentle reggae on the CD player and rolled herself a joint. She couldn't find a light, so she rummaged in the drawers next to the bed. A photo in a frame had been hidden underneath some clothes. She pulled it out and looked at it. It was of Oriel, a young black woman, and three small children. The woman was heart-stoppingly beautiful—even Orla could tell. She had wide, clear eyes and a bright smile and gazed confidently into the camera. Her hair looked expensively styled, falling in long waves to her shoulders. She was well dressed and glamorous, with cinnamon skin. To Orla, she looked perfect. She was all gloss, as if she was a guest on an American chat show giving life advice to the less well favoured. Orla just knew this was Oriel's wife, in reality if not in name. It was where he disappeared to. Though Orla didn't love him, she still felt tears pricking her eyes. It was amazing how Oriel always managed with women. He had charm for them in spite of all his rather obvious flaws. She didn't really understand it. She imagined that if she had the same effect on men that he had on women, her life would have been an easy ride. Orla had disrupted their world. Oriel was looking after her out of kindness, but really he should be with this woman and their children. She felt like she was a burden, a cuckoo in the nest. She didn't ever fit in, not ever. She lay back on the bed and smoked the joint. She wondered why life never seemed to sort itself out for her. Even though she did not love Oriel, she had envisaged making a life with him in this peaceful, relaxed place. Love might have grown again. Orla had felt they were almost making a strange sort of family: Oriel, Orla, and Benjamin.

But now there was this.

Oriel's other life.

How could she take him away from it?

Nothing ever worked out for Orla. She wondered if someone had cursed her long ago. She wondered if in another life she had done terrible things and this life was some karmic retribution. She had gone through a New Age phase and had read about reincarnation. It kind of made sense to her. She had to work some things out in this life to make up for wrongdoing in past lives. Orla supposed she had had chances to be a better person, but she had squandered them. She had given in to base passions when she should have been working on her spiritual development. So she was paying yet again with another lesson. She could not be happy with Oriel. She had been wild when she was young, but she didn't think she had ever been terribly bad. Yet she had never been happy, had never prospered.

Orla lay in the bed and drew the thin duvet around her, listening to the approaching storm. The carefully constructed mental world she had built over the last few weeks seemed to crash around her. The castle walls were breached, and the enemy was at the gate. Again. Orla didn't know what to do. There was no escape from herself. She felt like she ruined everything that she touched, everything that she tried to do. She got the bottle of rum from the cupboard and poured herself a large one. She then rolled another joint. She wanted not to feel so much. She needed to be calmer. Eventually, after several more shots of rum and sundry more joints, she drifted into a fitful sleep.

She couldn't escape from herself in dreams. There was Nathaniel, perfect Nathaniel with his perfect life. Orla felt herself reach for him, but he was always too far away, just out of reach. He was still smiling at her but so far away. Orla could see her hands reaching out to Nathaniel, but he didn't reach back. He just kept on smiling. Orla wasn't even sure if the smile was benign or if he was really laughing at her—had been laughing at her all along. He didn't reach back to her. Elijah lurched into her dream and took hold of her, leading her to the edge of the wood.

Then he disappeared.

There was an elderly lady standing at the edge of the wood. She was beckoning Orla, her wrinkled hands moving back and forth, willing Orla to come nearer. She was wearing a white apron over a pink floral-print dress and had the look of a kind of country grandmother who had just been baking cookies. She was like a grandma in an American 1950s comedy, everything a grandmother should be: grey hair swept untidily into a bun, kindly watery eyes, gentle ways, homeliness. Orla followed her into the wood. They came to a clearing. There was no sound at all: no birdsong, no buzzing of insects, no scuffling of creatures. Orla seemed to rise up high above the clearing. She didn't have a body. She could see everything. She saw Elijah lying on the grass with a small pistol lying at his side. There was dark blood pooling around his head, and half his forehead was missing. She could actually see part of his brain and skull. So much blood.

Orla woke and sat upright in the bed. Her eyes were staring wide with shock. The dream had been so vivid. Orla felt confusion. Her dreams had been wrong before and had led her into trouble. Some of the trouble she had had recently could be ascribed to Orla listening to her dreams.

But it had been so real.

She had seen Elijah so clearly. She could have reached out and touched his hair or smoothed his eyebrow. It was like he was really there. If it were true, she knew what it meant. He had shot himself. Why, she did not know. A cold thought was that it was something to do with her. She had caused harm to someone yet again. The horror of it hit her with the force of a blow. Her head felt like iron bands were wrapped around it. The coming storm seemed to be inside her head. She got up and paced the room. Thoughts jumbled in on her. Too many thoughts. Orla went to the drawer and got out the photo of Oriel's woman. She looked at it for several minutes.

Pain.

More pain.

That was all she seemed to have.

What could she do? She needed a solution. A cold plan crept into her mind. It would be better for Oriel if she wasn't there. It would be better for his wife. It would be better for his children. Nobody would miss her. Benjamin flitted into her mind. No. He would find another friend. He wouldn't miss her.

Nobody would miss her.

She didn't know why Elijah had shot himself, but she knew it was her fault. He had sent her a message. Had she ruined his life? Had she traumatised him? She didn't know. Orla felt she had no further use on earth. She had no job, no purpose, no meaningful human relationships. She had outlived her usefulness. She had ruined everything.

She knew what she had to do.

There was no other option.

All other roads were shut off.

Orla pulled on her beach kaftan, which reached above her knees, and forced some flip-flops on her feet. Ridiculously, she made the bed and tidied her things on the dresser. She didn't want to be any trouble to Oriel. She opened the door and crept into the corridor. She closed the door behind her as quietly as possible, careful not to be disturbed. She ran on light feet downstairs to the bar and then out into the street. The storm had gained force. The wind slapped into her back and propelled her forward. It was as if it was willing her down the beach. The universe was on her side. The rain was falling horizontally, soaking Orla. It felt cold and hard like whips. Orla ran with it until her feet hit the sand. The power was out. There was no light, only blackness, but she knew the way to the beach by instinct. The wind was screaming. All that Orla could hear was this sound. It was menacing—it meant to kill, to destroy anything it passed. She ran forward to the shoreline. She slipped her feet out of the flip-flops and flung her kaftan to the side. She raised her arms above her head and stared into the blackness in front of her. She was not afraid. She felt total calm. She was convinced of the rightness of what she was about to do. She had always wanted to help people, but she would be more help dead than alive. There was a poison in her that ruined everything. She wanted Oriel to be happy, and without her there to ruin his life, he could be. He would not have to feel duty towards her anymore.

Orla had a dim idea of what the afterlife would be, but she hoped there was something. She would not have to endure the indescribable pain of the past hour. There would be no pain. Even if there was nothing, there would be no pain. Orla hoped there would be something. Some way of making it all right—some possibility for atonement. She was so tired of feeling.

She walked into the sea.

There was the unusual coldness of the water lapping at her thighs, then her breasts, then her chin. She lost footing on the sand beneath her feet and her head submerged. The water enfolded her as in a womb. An ancient stirring of survival surged in her, and her feet kicked her upwards while her arms curved to make her swim. Orla's mind flashed to school swimming lessons and how bad she had been. Her bone-thin arms and legs had never been any use to her. Orla smiled; she could use her useless body against herself. She would not be able to swim for long. She swam out farther and farther until her arms ached and ached. There seemed to be no time. Orla had no idea how long she had been swimming. Her body gave up. She sank into the water. There was more blackness. The water filled her mouth and then her lungs, diving deep inside her. Her chest felt as if it would burst open. There was intense pain inside her. Then it stopped. There was no pain. There was calm and peace welling up inside her, cradling her as if she was in enormous arms.

A voice she couldn't place seemed to be in her head…and also not in it.

"Everything will be all right, Orla. Everything is all right."

White light was all around her, impossibly bright.

There was her own grandmother in the light with her grey hair and her lined face but her eyes dancing with happiness.

"Go back, Orla. You must go back."

"No, Oma, no. I want to stay with you."

Orla remembered the German name she had called her grandmother as a child. She was a child again in the garden of the old, grey house in Peterhead, watering the roses with a plastic yellow can.

"No, Orla. You never listened. You never listened to anyone. You were a wild thing. You must go back. You have so much more to do."

Her Oma's eyes were still shining with merriment as she shook her head at Orla as if she were still an errant child.

Then there was Elijah standing a distance away from her, looking down as if embarrassed to meet her gaze. He was not as in the dream but perfectly restored, as beautiful as he had ever been. He raised his eyes to meet hers, and she felt her hands reaching to touch his face.

"Orla, you have to understand. It wasn't my fault. It wasn't me. Forgive me. You have to go back. I'll be here. I'll always be here."

Orla could feel as if she were him. She could feel his desperation for her forgiveness and an exquisite feeling of love that was like a pain, though it was also pleasure. But for Orla, there was nothing to forgive. She couldn't remember anything bad. She only felt happiness and a serenity she had never felt before in her life.

It was like coming home after a long walk.

CHAPTER TWENTY-THREE

Orla woke. Her face felt like wood. She opened one eye gingerly and then another. Her tongue explored her lips, which were roughly cracked and salty. Her body ached all over. She wasn't sure if she could move. She tried to raise her head and then let it drop down again.

She had a sickening realisation: she was still alive. She had even failed to commit suicide. The irony of this made her start to laugh, but laughing caused pain in her chest and ribs, so she stopped herself. How could she not have died? She remembered dying, remembered drowning. What miracle had kept her alive?

She was dimly aware that she was floating on a wooden pallet in the ocean. It was bright daylight and calm. The bobbing of the wood was restful.

She could hear a voice calling her name. "Orla! Orla! Orla!"

She thought the voice was inside her head. *I am still bloody mad*, she thought.

She felt hands reaching under her arms, and after a few moments' struggle, they turned her over, and she crashed back onto the wood with a thud.

It was Benjamin.

His face was contorted into worry.

"Orla, Orla, are you alive? Orla, Orla!"

She managed to smile up at him, and seeing this, his face lit up with delight.

"Orla, Orla. You can't die. You have to live. You have to be my mother. You have to look after me. I look after you. I love you. Forever and ever. Amen."

"Yes," she replied, "yes, forever and ever."

In spite of the pain in her chest, Orla laughed and laughed. She felt tears running down her face, and her eyes smarted.

The perfectly circular orange sun beat its rays impassively into Benjamin and Orla.

Yes. Orla still had much to do.

Made in the USA
Charleston, SC
02 August 2016